THE DEAD
BEAR WITNESS

Other titles by James Chambers
The Engines of Sacrifice
Resurrection House
On the Night Border

Other eSpec Books Titles
by James Chambers

The Corpse Fauna Series
(forthcoming)
Tears of Blood
The Dead in Their Masses
The Eyes of the Dead

Other eSpec Books Titles
including James Chambers

After Punk:
Steampowered Tales of the Afterlife

The Side of Good/The Side of Evil

Gaslight & Grimm

Dogs of War
Man and Machine
In Harm's Way
Best of Defending the Future

If We Had Known
Footprints in the Stars

Best of Bad-Ass Faeries

Society for the Preservation
of CJ Henderson

Corpse Fauna
Volume One

JAMES CHAMBERS

THE DEAD BEAR WITNESS

NEOPARADOXA
PENNSVILLE, NJ

PUBLISHED BY
NeoParadoxa
a division of eSpec Books LLC
Danielle McPhail,
Publisher
PO Box 242,
Pennsville, New Jersey 08070
www.especbooks.com

ISBN: 978-1-942990-99-4
ISBN (eBook): 978-1-942990-76-5

Earlier versions of "The Dead Bear Witness" appeared in a chapbook published by Die, Monster, Die! Books, 2002; *The Dead Walk.* Vincent Sneed, ed. Baltimore, MD: Die, Monster, Die! Books, 2004; and *The Dead Bear Witness*, Dark Quest Books, Howell, NJ, 2012.

"Birch's Refugees" was previously published in *The Dead Bear Witness,* Dark Quest Books, Howell, NJ, 2012.

All persons, places, and events in this book are fictitious and any resemblance to actual persons, places, or events is purely co-incidental.

Copy Editor: Greg Schauer

Interior Design: Danielle McPhail,
Sidhe na Daire Multimedia
www.sidhenadaire.com

Interior Art: Jason Whitley
Cover Art: Glen Ostrander
Cover Design: Mike McPhail, McP Digital Graphics

CONTENTS

For Chris and Vince,
walking dead men
till the end

THE DEAD BEAR WITNESS

CORNELL:
ONE

Four guys committed suicide today. One managed to do the job right.

A wiry kid in for possession doused his clothes in turpentine from the shop, then set a match to his shirt. The screws displayed uncharacteristically good sense letting him burn a while so he wouldn't rise up again after they hit him with fire extinguishers.

Another made a grab for a guard's gun, forcing a shootout. The hacks fought his corpse into submission long enough to set fire to it.

Number three swallowed most of a box of rat poison, told no one, and died on his feet washing breakfast dishes in the kitchen. He bit through the throat of the inmate next to him before the other cons cleared out, and two guards returned with scatterguns to rip the dead bastards to pieces.

The fourth grabbed a knife during lunch and cut his own throat. Panicked inmates stumbled over each other trying to get away, blocking the screws from reaching the body before it switched on again. He killed two more inmates and wounded a guard before they pinned down all four of them and dragged them to the infirmary for chopping up.

Nightmare fuel that made me homesick for solitary.

I'd spent a month there only to emerge into the devil's definition of a life-and-death struggle, and I honestly could not say which side I preferred.

My stint in the hole came by way of punishment for breaking the collarbone of some Aryan Brotherhood asshole who wanted to "protect" me. Show no weakness to those white supremacist fucks—they *will* make you their dog or kill you trying. Warden Lane Grove knew it as well as I did, but I was fresh blood and a media darling, and he wanted to teach me a lesson about getting cocky.

Last thing the warden told me before he slammed shut the cell door was, "You think you're someone special, son? Someone different and unique? You're nobody special. You're only clay like all the rest of us. Sooner you accept that, better off you'll be, because if you think my punishment is harsh, you'll find an even ruder surprise waiting for you in the next world if you don't change your ways."

Worst thing for me about solitary was that there was nothing to occupy my mind but thinking about how horribly I had screwed up when I was on top of the world. They wouldn't allow me my books or even a Walkman—nothing but the searing brightness of the cell's single bare bulb lit twenty-four, seven. That and all the time I needed to pick over the carcass of my memories, like the last time I saw Evelyn or the look on the bank manager's face when three slugs from my Beretta M9 bored through his gut. Sometimes I got to wondering how it might have gone if I'd been just a few seconds faster.

That's when I came to understand what Evelyn meant when she used to say the world is a smiling jackal eager for its chance to tear out your throat and lap up your blood. Most people don't see it coming for the clutter in their lives, like politics or religion or trying to make a decent living with the deck stacked against them. Evelyn and I never had much use for all those things telling people the "right" way to live. Better to take what we needed and be long gone when the man came around to collect his due.

I believe Evelyn held to that right up to the moment I dropped my guard and got her and our baby growing inside her killed.

TWO

When my four weeks in isolation ended, Officer Paulson and Officer Gamewood yanked me out of the hole and dragged me down the hall to the infirmary, while I chased dime-sized ghost glares burned onto my retinas by the bulb in my cell. Wasted from hunger and not having slept more than an hour at a time since they tossed me down there, I wasn't so far gone I didn't notice Paulson's sickly tremors or the glistening film of sweat coating his pale face, or how he mumbled into the empty air, not talking to me or anyone else really.

"Whole world's over. End of everything," he said.

I figured the whole thing was a sick joke, a head game, more of my continuing education according to Lane Grove. Or maybe Paulson liked to get a little high on the job. Had second thoughts about all that after the horror show at the infirmary.

While I lay on a gurney with an IV of saline solution plugged into my arm to treat me for dehydration, a couple of hacks brought in Sammy Costa, ashen-faced and bleeding like a New York City fire hydrant in July. He was a snub-nosed car-thief on a ten-year chip for his third strike. He was a stupid man with a smart mouth. So, it was no surprise someone had decided to slice him open and make good work of it. The guards hefted him onto the gurney beside mine, but the two-foot wide puddle of blood that Sammy's wounds spilled onto the floor made it obvious there was no saving him. Doctor Foley took one look, shook his head, and called the time of death. Then he set to work with the nurse and guards ripping Sammy apart like the devil's pit crew.

They used bright scalpels and whirring bone saws. Blood spattered and flesh tore. Muscle snapped like strands of aged chewing gum. Translucent flaps of skin peeled back from bone and sinew. Joints cracked, and foul patches of gas belched from the recesses of Costa's body. His left arm came loose and a guard dropped it into a thick vinyl bag, sealed the bag shut, and tossed it into a waiting laundry cart. Next went Sammy's legs, each one amputated below the knee, wrapped in separate containers then tossed on the pile. Every few seconds the nurse called out the time, counting it down. Sweat dripped from Doctor Foley's face.

It mixed with Costa's blood and ran in milky rivulets along the doctor's silver tools.

Costa's right arm vanished into a plastic sack.

Guards yanked on his thighs and spread them until his hip joints surrendered with a loud snap.

"One minute," the nurse said.

Thirty seconds later they finished. Foley hunched over Costa's face, sliced a scalpel through what was left of his neck, and then wrenched the car thief's head free from his body. Two guards slipped a body bag over his torso; another held one open for the head. All that was enough to make me think I'd died in the hole and woken up in some insane hellish version of reality, but then as Sammy's lifeless, gray face vanished into black plastic, his smartass eyes flicked open and stared right at me. They gleamed like polished ivory in the last beam of light that touched them. They were cool as December, like all was right in Sammy's world. Soon as that bagged head crowned the pile of body parts, the aluminum cart shimmied and rattled. Slow at first, like when a truck rolls by a house and shakes the pictures on the walls, but then each black bundle wriggled, shifted around, twisted and turned like a caged rat. The canvas liner bulged as the severed limbs squirmed around each other.

The nurse screamed "Incinerator, now!" and sent the guards rushing the cart from the room.

The infirmary air swelled with the foul odor of raw flesh and the pungent stink of sleepless terror. I'm well acquainted with the scent of fear. It's a mixture of clean, dried sweat and the kind of body odor that comes from an adrenaline rush. Except for being so depleted by my hitch in solitary, I would've caught it wafting off my escort. I would've gagged on it rising from the medical staff when I entered the room. But it took the icy dread of seeing Sammy Costa ripped apart to make me realize fear's choking perfume tainted the entire prison. Now that I'd scented it, I couldn't ditch it.

I grabbed the nurse by the arm. Her nametag read Oberon. My voice came out like a rasp scratching across oak. "What in holy hell was that all about?"

"Shit," the nurse said. "You been living in a cave for the last month?"

THREE

Later, with a clean bill of health—aside from dehydration, sleep deprivation, malnourishment, and the general stress that comes from existing in a windowless three-by-five cell for a month—they sent me back into general population.

It was afternoon recreation period, so I went to the television room. It was empty. That time of day, the place should have been full of soap opera fans, but there was nothing but snow on every channel. I stretched out on the couch and relished its coarse comfort. I rested my eyes in the cool stillness of the room. Visions of Sammy Costa flashed through my mind, mixed with Nurse Oberon's weary eyes, and the sickly look on Paulson's face. I tried to pinpoint the exact moment when sanity had deserted the world. I couldn't do it.

Footsteps scuffed the tile floor. I shot upright and opened my eyes. A long-timer called Old Corntooth waved me back down and then shuffled to the table by the sofa. He sat on its corner and gave me the once over. I'd seen him around a few times, one of those guys who's been inside so long, he's like a ghost. He smiled, showing me how he'd earned his name.

"Been in solitary, ain't you?" he said. "You're out of touch, I suppose. Don't know the score anymore. Bad way to be in here. Uninformed, I mean. Lot's changed in a little time. You ought to watch this."

He handed me an unlabeled DVD in a clear plastic case.

"Television signals died two weeks back. All we's got left is a DVD-DVR machine in here. Got a couple of old football games up on the shelf, a couple of musicals, one of them Adam Sandler movies, but this here's the only one you need. It's the only one that means much. When you're done, stick it in the crack between the wall and the cabinet. I'll fetch it later. We ain't supposed to have it, y'know? Warden don't like this to circulate."

Old Corntooth left the room without looking back. I stared at the square of shining plastic in my hand, the silver circle inside it. Wasn't unusual for contraband skin flicks or movies the warden deemed objectionable to circulate in secret, but no one was likely to waste their time singling me out for something like that. Couldn't think of a good reason anyone might single me out at all. It's best in prison when no one pays any attention to you whatsoever. I wondered who'd sent it, knowing by the broken-down look in Old Corntooth's eyes that he'd never have bothered with me on his own.

I slid the disc into the player and sat back.

What followed: Two hours of raw, fucking chaos.

One-hundred and twenty minutes of madness.

Seventy-two-hundred seconds of death, blood, and blind panic.

That's what this movie was about.

The plot was shit, but the rest of it was convincing as all get-out. Someone had recorded it all while channel surfing and news channel or not, every damn broadcast was the same: the corpses of the dead now rose within four to ten minutes of death and hunted the living with a savageness of insane dimension. It was worst in the cities where mobs of the dead swarmed the streets, but inside a few of days it had spread everywhere. The corpses moved with desperate purpose, heedless of their own safety, ignorant of any injury, and their growing numbers replaced the lost two to one. Nothing stopped them but fire or cutting them to pieces. The hunger so clear in their blank eyes drove them to consume the thing they'd once been: the living.

The reporters all asked the same question, "Why?"

Sure enough there were theories: radiation, disease, voodoo, parasites, the Apocalypse, Wi-Fi, genetically modified tomatoes, RFID chips, iPad mind control apps, and on, and on. No one had figured it out by whatever day the broadcasts had been recorded. Not that it mattered. The people on television worried about stopping it before it was too late, but it seemed like that point had come and gone and caught everyone with their pants down.

Except for me.

I got to watch the whole thing as if it was taking place right then. I pictured people outside fighting for survival against the mobs of walking dead. I thought of cities packed with panicked crowds, hospitals overrun with corpses that wouldn't stay down, and roads choked by cars, trucks, and useless ambulances. My imagination ran away a touch, I admit, but I've always been that way. Thing was, what all the other men had experienced over the past weeks, locked up helpless inside while the rest of the world died, I put myself through in two hours, catching up fast. And I understood that all that was in the past, that with the dead spreading as fast the reporters said, any frantic battles for life were all over and decided by now. What had been a month in the hole for me must have seemed like years to the people outside. And that bastard Grove had let me stay there to rot as if the end of it all was no concern of mine, as if I were the ultimate outsider, living in my own world. Maybe he was right.

The DVD ended with a blank blue screen that matched the empty patch in my memory from my time in the hole. Damn video did wonders for my doubts about my sanity.

We'd been safely locked up, a thing for which not a man among us would have been grateful five weeks ago. And I wondered how many felt differently now. What was there to look forward to after we did our time: families, homes, girlfriends, money? Shit, some of us had lost all of that long before resurrection fever began firing up the dead. They say there's nothing more dangerous than a man with nothing left to lose, and here I was penned up with a prison full of men, nothing in any of our futures but rot and darkness. I almost wished I'd never been dragged out of my rational, little cube in solitary.

FOUR

Hit the exercise yard to shock my muscles out of the atrophy of confinement. Physical exertion clears my head. I had a hunch I was going to need my wits as much as my strength soon.

Outside was cool and dry, the kind of spring weather that makes you want to drive a hundred miles an hour with the top down. For half a heartbeat I wondered if the world had really changed. Here it was: alive and untouched for all I could see, free of nightmares other than the ones we bring to life ourselves. Then I smelled the lingering odor of decay in the air and heard the low undercurrent of voices echoing in the yard, coming not from the prisoners but from outside the prison walls. Rifle reports snapped from the perimeter stations at irregular intervals. The gunshots mingled with the crash of hammers. At one end of the yard, workers were erecting a structure with lumber that had been meant for the new storage shed. A hill of old junk and debris was piled up beside it.

I settled onto the bench and began pumping through my first set. The heft of the barbell laced strands of pain through my chest, but the grimy iron felt good in my hands. A con came over to spot me, looking grateful for the break in his boredom. He smoked a cigarette while I went through two more sets. My muscles warmed to the exertion with the last one, so I switched to smaller weights and kept at it, boiling off the cold dread gathered at the base of my spine. I worked my body until the knots in my gut melted to nothing, and then I sat there panting while the breeze licked the sweat from my back.

That's when Klug approached me, stopping here and there along the way to bum a drag off someone's smoke, gab with other cons, or tie his shoe, the whole time keeping his eyes on me with a gaze like a stream of ice water. Coming slow so as not to scare me but letting me know I'd better sit tight and wait for him.

Klug was near seven-feet tall and built like a linebacker, big with much more muscle than fat. His clean-shaven head glistened in the sunlight. A bright cobra hood tattoo adorned the back of his neck and skull. Nobody fucked with the King Snake. There was no point. Not a man in the yard could take him one-on-one, and Klug, for his part, liked his privacy. A genuine live-and-let-live arrangement, which from what I could see, worked fine. Klug had been high up on the food chain before the cops brought him low on a bogus firearms charge, and he went inside with solid connections. Even the supercops kissed his ass. Klug returned the favor by using his influence to help maintain order when it suited him. That kind of shit made for easy time, I suppose, but shots like Klug do you a favor just to obligate you. My first day in I'd elected to do everything possible to stay off his radar.

Guess I screwed the pooch on that plan. Klug stepped up beside me, and the temperature dropped three degrees in his shadow.

"Hear you're a Lohatchie boy," he said.

"Yeah?" I asked. "Where'd you hear that?"

"Don't much matter. I grew up in Lohatchie, too. Spent my summers playing around the 'Glades, running airboats for Gator Joe's. Lived down on Kettrick by the rail yard till I left when I was sixteen. You look about the right age. Imagine we might have passed each other on the street more than once."

"Probably did. Gator Joe's went out of business long time ago, you know."

"I heard. Too bad about that. Joe deserved better than the shit he wound up eating."

A flurry of gunshots crackled on the wind. Klug craned his neck, intent on the vibrant sky like he was waiting for the answer to some unspoken question. Behind his careful expression his eyes hinted at the rapid-fire thoughts gamboling through his mind. Whether or not the answer ever came to him, I don't know, but he met my gaze again and put a hand on my arm, squeezing the muscle tight.

"Waste of good ammo," he said. "Nothing stops them short of incineration or blowing them into very small, very immobile bits. Slice them apart, their arms and legs will come after you as best they can. We're lucky the fuckers are so slow and stupid."

I thought of Sammy, a man in pieces, still kicking.

"Old Corntooth told me he showed you the news, so you know what's what now," Klug said. "Could be we're the only ones left, I suppose. Likely there are others out there in situations like ours, but there's no way to know. Ain't no real communications left working. Warden Grove carried things on like normal for a few days, but when it was clear this thing wasn't going to turn around, he locked us down drum tight. No one in, no one out, no exceptions. Not even the guards' families. The screws looked ready to mutiny at one point, but Grove kept enough of them loyal to hold the lid on. Pretty soon they all realized that whatever family they'd left behind would probably best be forgotten. So, now, except that they got all the guns, they're prisoners here, too, like us."

"I'm tickled by the irony."

Klug cracked what might have been a smile, but I wouldn't swear to it.

"You ever eat down at Mona and Joan's on Banyan?"

"More than a few times," I said. "Damn good fries."

"Yeah. And milkshakes. Nothing beat their chocolate shakes."

"Screw chocolate. Strawberry-banana. Joan's specialty. The ultimate shake."

"Shit, I'd fight my way through a dozen men for one of those right now." Klug smiled for sure this time, parting his lips and licking his broad white teeth like he could taste the food right then—golden crisp and steeped in oil and salt, sugar sweet and creamy cold. "Yeah, it's good to be talking to a Lohatchie boy. Man, I bet we're the last two left. Funny us both winding up here. Especially since word is you got a place in the wilderness down there, where if you'd have made it before the Feds caught up with you, they might not have caught you at all."

That knocked the wind out of me. I couldn't imagine how Klug or anyone else here knew about that.

Klug read my expression.

"I been in here long enough, I can tell you not to expend a lot of energy keeping secrets. It ain't possible, least not from me."

"Suppose it's true. So what? It'd have to be hundreds of miles away from this shithole, from anywhere, in fact, wouldn't it?"

"Most of this sorry lot in here haven't caught on yet to the warden's grand plan." Klug paused to light a clove cigarette and exhaled a sweetly acrid cloud over my head. "Understand this: That man will see to it none of us ever leaves this prison alive. We have provisions stockpiled for another week, maybe two if they get stingy, and we got generators for power, but fuel is running low. He can't keep us here long without thinning the population or recruiting men to forage for supplies. He doesn't have enough guards to send any away scavenging, and he sure as hell won't trust any of the cons to do it. He knows—walking dead or not—they'd never come back once he let them outside the walls.

"Even if he could make a go of it, he wouldn't bother. When the dead began to walk Grove declared it the End of Days. He curled up squarely in the pages of his Bible and he hasn't come out since. We all had to find some way to cope. The ones that didn't aren't around anymore. For a man like Grove, with that big a hard-on for God to begin with, this has got to seem like some seriously momentous shit. Protecting us is keeping us from God's righteous judgment. Sealing us up in here to ride out the storm would be holding us back from the world as the Lord hath remade it. So, he won't let anyone out to hunt or try to find out what's happening. We could be living like princes here, but he lets the wormfeeders collect up around the walls because he believes most of us are meant to die at their hands. It's just a matter of time before he decides to throw open the doors and let us all get cozy with God's latest plague upon humanity."

"Why hasn't he done it already?"

"Wants to prepare us before we go, make sure we repent our sins and all that happy horseshit. A few of us have decided to be elsewhere when this particular shit hits the fan. The wormfeeders go where the food is, meaning where we are. There must be six, seven hundred outside, scattered around the countryside, pressing at the gates, homing in on us. Ten, fifteen, twenty more show up every day. From where I don't know because the nearest town is thirty miles away. They're damn tough to kill, and they make more of themselves fast. Couple weeks back a busload of people came banging at the door. Grove refused them entrance then ordered the guards to open fire. The ones killed by bullets got up and started eating the live ones. Fifteen minutes later, the whole lot of them had joined the big dead party."

"Break out and where do you run?" I said. "You figure if you can get far enough away, maybe someplace like my alleged hideaway, they won't pick up the scent."

"Scent, noise, psychic vibration, whatever the fuck they get off on. Got to be a limit to their range. That's my theory, anyway. Figure I'm better off out there testing it than rotting in here waiting to die."

"What if I'm not interested?"

Mild surprise ran through Klug's face. "I hadn't considered that. I will if you really need an answer."

I shook my head. "Leaving here sounds fine. How many?"

"Nine, including you and me."

"Too many. Needs to be less when we get where we're going. It ain't exactly a mansion."

"Well, such things have a way of working themselves out." Klug took a last drag on his cigarette, dropped it to the ground, and stamped it out. "I know I can trust you to keep this quiet, Lohatchie boy. Tonight, after Grove's dog-and-pony show, go back to your cell, wait one hour, then meet me in the cafeteria. It's been arranged."

Klug blended into the crowd. Another burst of faraway gunshots ripped through the afternoon.

Feeling exposed and weak in the hot sun, I watched the men work away building the structure. Feverish chills ran through my body. I feared I was coming down sick, but then I realized I was shivering because I'd recognized what Warden Grove was constructing down the yard.

He was having a gallows built.

FIVE

I sat alone at supper.

It was a pleasant change.

My first day in, everyone had wanted a piece of me. They had seen me on the news for weeks: "the modern-day John Dillinger," the bank-robbing folk hero who relied more on his wits than his gun and made monkeys out of the cops. Yeah, it was a healthy dose of exaggeration, but there was some truth in it, too. I robbed more than a dozen banks over two years and came away clean with more cash than Joe Six-pack could make in a decade worth of overtime. Still got a fair amount of cash safely stashed, all of it about as valuable as dirt in the current state of the world. When I did a bank I did it in style, and I did it smart. Jumped from state to state, kept a low profile, used a different crew each time, different methods, wore disguises, did everything I could to erase my signature. I enjoyed a fair amount of luck, too; whenever I was on the job things seemed to break my way more often than not. Simple things, like a guard taking an unscheduled bathroom break, or the bank not being full of customers, or hitting all green lights on the way out of town. Little things made a difference when it came to a clean getaway.

I hit nine banks before anyone connected the first four. Most of them had been fast, in and out, grabs off the tellers, but the time could be stretched, maybe take some of the vault, and I did that a few times for the big hauls. It wasn't hard with Evelyn on my side. Girl like her made information easy to come by, so we could go in on the guard's coffee break or avoid banks that rigged cash with GPS chips and dye bombs and marked bills.

The best part—at least until my last job—was no one ever got hurt. That lone fact had a good portion of the public on my side by the day the news broke that the Feds had connected all my robberies, admitting in the process that they'd been outsmarted for a solid eighteen months. I won over even more people by the time they caught me, having accomplished some conspicuous good deeds with portions of the take. Call it buying good publicity, because that's what it was. Mug for the camera, flash a nice smile, let them see you're just an average guy, and it reminds them all how much they'd like to buck the system the same way you did if they only had the balls and the smarts. That's the beauty of mass communication. Blur the lines enough then real life vanishes and people think they're watching a movie. Bank robber? No, sir, not me! I'm the next great, misunderstood, anti-hero "victim of a heartless society driven to a life of desperate crime." I was a modern-day Robin Hood driving a late model Lexus SUV, proving anyone can have anything they want if they only have the stones to take it. Even the most law-abiding drones respond to that with hope and envy, if only on a subconscious level. When the Feds caught me, though, I was still reeling from losing Evelyn. Hell, I got more than a thousand consolation cards while I was on ice waiting for my trial, plus half a dozen offers to go on talk shows and tell my side of events so "the people could understand." All they really wanted was to pick me apart like a new toy that fascinated them as much as it disgusted them.

None of that crap interested me.

I missed Evelyn too much. I thought I deserved to suffer for letting her down so I pled guilty.

The court handed me a life sentence for killing the bank manager and two security guards. My public defender threw his arms up in frustration at me copping to a rap he thought we could beat down to manslaughter. Only thing that kept the needle out of my arm was a spark of mercy fanned by the fact that one of the men I killed had just shot my pregnant wife to death. The model definition of a "fucked-up chain of events," I suppose.

And consider this: if I'd walked, or kept myself tied up in court on appeal, I'd probably be dead now, tromping around rotting in the sun.

Tempts me to start believing in fate.

Let me assure you, though, that it's a bad thing to come into stir with a reputation of any kind. Others feel duty-bound to take you down a peg or two, see if you got any real juice. That made my life difficult at best until I lost my cool with that skinhead punk. While I was in the hole, word had traveled about what I had done to get there. That told everyone else—except people like Klug—to keep their distance. My first night back no one seemed itchy for a scrap. The whole cafeteria was so damn subdued it made my skin crawl, and I knew it was those wooden beams raised above the prison courtyard that dominated the thoughts every of man around me. We were to assemble in the yard for a special service following dinner. Warden Grove's orders. They hadn't strung the ropes before mealtime, but we all knew they'd be hung in time for the night's activities.

Old Corntooth parked himself beside me as I sucked down a forkful of red Jell-O.

"Klug got you, huh? Shots like him usually get what they want," he said.

"Don't know what you're talking about, old timer."

"Uh-huh." His railroad track smile faded. "I'll tell you the same thing I told Klug. Skip it. It ain't gonna happen. You're better off here, cause no matter what they throw at you, you can always find a way to keep your head down and tough it out. You try and force 'em to play by your rules, they just going to smash you down. I been in near thirty years, and I know what I'm talking about."

"You don't even know what time it is. This play is for everything. Keeping a low profile ain't going to save your skinny ass this time. But maybe an old fart like you ain't too concerned about that."

I dropped my spoon and broke Old Corntooth's grip where he'd clutched my wrist. He poked a finger against my chest.

"I'm supposed to be out in six months. You hear me? Then I go free, I get my life back, and this shit has to go down, now." He coughed. Tears welled in his drooping eyes. "You and Klug and them, you all carrying on like it ain't nothing. It ain't fair."

I felt the supercops' eyes checking up on us, so I stood up to leave, lingering long enough to whisper, "What's changed, old man? The world is full of empty-headed bodies colliding off each other the way it always was. Gotta find an angle and make it work for you. Give up fighting and you're like those bastards outside: dead. Most of the ones out there—hell, most *in* here— were dead a long time ago. Only they were too fucking stupid to lie down and stop breathing."

Corntooth shook his head. "No, no, it ain't like that."

I pushed past the old man as gentle as I could and left him with his shoulders sagging like a week-old balloon. A crowd began filtering out to the yard, and I had gotten my fill of the somber efficiency of the cafeteria. I wanted to raise my eyes and see stars instead of a greasy stone ceiling for a change. I followed the others into the rose-amber glow of the raging bonfire that now consumed the junk pile beside the gallows. I stood in the shadow of a watchtower manned, as they all were, by men with automatic rifles. The firelight made the sky hazy, but I picked out enough stars to satisfy me. Fifteen, twenty minutes ticked off before everyone was gathered there, grim-faced, determined not to betray the slightest bit of fear but failing. A crowd that big keeping that quiet unnerved me. I scanned around for Klug but caught no sign of him.

Thundering music exploded from the loudspeakers, slow and funereal, some God-awful classical shit that filled us with a sense of powerlessness. Warden Grove possessed quite a touch of showmanship, having once been a revivalist preacher, and he played the part well. Ten figures marched onto the platform: three inmates bound in shackles, escorted by two shotgun-toting hacks apiece. A stocky, dark-suited man with his mouth hidden behind a blue surgeon's mask followed them; no question, he was an executioner. One-by-one the cons took their places below the gallows poles, all three of which now hung with coarse ropes tied in nooses that swayed a little in the breeze.

Warden Grove entered like a prince deigning to address his frightened subjects. The bastard telegraphed everything there was I hated about people like him.

"I will waste no time, men." He spoke into his microphone, and his voice boomed from the public address system. "Time is now more truly of the essence than ever before in life. Now it is the hour and the day of the master's return, and if you have not kept your house in order, then let this be your last chance to put your soul right. Tonight, three sinners stand beside me, gazed upon by a host of sinners. We all are sinners in the eyes of God. All of you, to the last man, bend beneath the weight of your guilt. I see it, men. I do. It burdens you like foul mud staining the fabric of your spirit. The Good Book promises that on judgment day there will be a reckoning, and on that day the dead shall rise from their graves. That day is at hand. No longer can you afford the luxury of your craven ways. It's time to repent as these three brave souls behind me have done."

Grove poked the microphone toward the first inmate's face. "Your name, son?" he said.

The man was so beaten and bruised he could only stand propped up by his escort. Grove shoved the microphone closer.

"Again, son. Your name?"

"Donnie...uh, Don Cooper," he said.

"What path have you chosen, Mr. Cooper?"

"God's path. I've chosen to...repent my sins. To go to the Lord...with a clear conscience."

"The Lord has forgiven you, Mr. Cooper, as he is willing to forgive all sinners. Now that you've taken God into your heart, it's left to you to see that your soul remains in its current state of grace, that you don't backslide and once again become one of the fallen. Would you do me the humble honor of accepting my assistance in assuring this?"

"Yeah...uh, yes, please," said Cooper, struggling as if to remember lines.

Grove asked the same questions of the other two men and got the same canned answers, though none of them looked like they understood what was happening. They'd all been pounded hard, broken down, and driven to submission. They would have agreed to almost anything only to put an end to whatever Grove had been doing to them.

"God so loved Mankind, he gave unto us his only Son, and sacrificed him for our sins," Grove said. "It is our duty to follow his example, by sacrificing ourselves to redeem our tainted spirits. These men are here tonight as examples for you all, guides to show you the way to light, truth, and salvation."

The executioner draped velvet hoods over the head of each supplicant and fitted nooses around their necks.

"Donny?" one of the men called. "Donny, I can't see you. What's happening?"

"It's okay, Arthur. I'm still here, and this shit…this shit is almost over. You just…keep your head together," said Cooper, his voice muffled by his hood.

"Men, pray now for your fellows that their souls might find peace," said Grove.

"Donny!" the con screamed.

The executioner sprang the trap doors. The three convicts dropped into air. The sound of their necks snapping seemed small and insufficient for such a terrible thing. Their bodies dangled, bobbing and swaying like mute wind chimes. I'd never seen a man hang before, and I'll tell you it's not quick and clean like they show it in the movies. Matter of fact, it's a damn messy, nasty way to die, unless it's done to perfection. And how often does perfection happen in this world?

Quiet reigned a long time over the crowd. The crackling of the fire was the only sound to be heard aside from the moans of the restless dead traveling on the wind. A number of men looked at their watches, some stared at their shoes. Everyone knew what was coming. No one stirred. A few minutes passed, and then the corpses jerked to life with clumsy, sweeping kicks. They wind-milled their arms like marionettes, and in the firelight, it looked like they were dancing in air to some slow music only they could hear. Grove let the show go on awhile. Later a bunch of hacks came and took position above each hanging body, three to a man.

"The unrepentant man is doomed to eternal flesh and carnal punishment," said Warden Grove. "Such is the fate of the worldly. Only those who choose forgiveness may transcend to a higher existence."

The screws hauled the flailing bodies up, each grabbing a limb or two, while another yanked the noose free. I was grateful for not having to see the dead men's blank eyes beneath their hoods, for knowing they couldn't see the rage and horror in our faces if they could see such things at all anymore.

"Free these men of their flesh!" Grove shouted.

The guards heaved the first of the struggling bodies onto the bonfire. It burned slow like green wood and wet leather, as it kicked and burrowed deeper into the trash heap. The others followed. All three tunneled their way toward the heart of the conflagration like they were drawn to the heat at its center. Disgusted cries and impotent curses rose from the crowd.

"These men have been saved and their souls are set free." Warden Grove swelled with pride. "Who would like to be next?"

I never before heard a silence like the one that answered him; it was heavy and hard and full of hot shock and burning hatred like a firestorm waiting to gush down and incinerate everything it touched.

"Men, I anticipated your reluctance to join the ranks of the saved tonight. To resolve spiritual matters often requires preparation and deep contemplation. I understand. So this will now be part of our daily routine, until each man among you worthy of saving has made his peace with the Lord and been safely sent to his eternal reward. Remain here for one hour. Reflect upon what you have seen. Then you are to return to your cells. Those of you who choose salvation may tell any prison official at any time in order for the appropriate arrangements to be made."

Grove descended the platform and disappeared inside, leaving us to perspire for sixty minutes in the warm night and the heat of the bonfire. Within the flames, the three corpses grew thin and black until not a scrap of flesh remained on their charred bones.

Then, finally, they ceased to move.

SIX

Later I lay in my cell, thinking how smart my pedophile cellmate, Baldwin, was to leave me undisturbed. On my third day inside, after catching him using my comb, I'd promised to make sure he didn't live to see the end of summer. Can't say I really meant it, as repugnant as he was, but the threat stopped him from interfering with me or my things.

I worked at reading the tattered copy of *The Subterraneans* I'd gotten from the prison library before being dumped in solitary, but mostly I stared at the ceiling or glanced at my watch, waiting for the hour to pass. When it was almost time, I dropped to the floor, snaked my hand into the narrow space between the metal leg of the bunk and the wall, and tapped until a loose chunk of masonry slipped free. A beat-up paperback of Faulkner's Light in August waited wedged inside. Hidden within it, where I had hollowed out some pages, was the jagged half of a snapped penknife blade, bound with duct tape to part of a wooden spoon handle. It wasn't much, but it was all I'd had time to acquire before my stint downstairs. I slipped it into the waistband of my shorts, enjoying the nervous glance Baldwin flashed at the sight of me with a shiv in my hand.

Sickly-looking Paulson came by on his rounds, pausing at my cell to unlock the door. He tipped me a nod then went on his way. I waited a minute before I crept out. I ignored the hatred and envy that poured from of the eyes of the insomniac men in the other cells. Any one of them would've been glad to trade places with me as the King Snake's new favorite. I reached the end of the cellblock and walked deeper into the prison. Along the way, I passed three guard stations, each one deserted. I encountered no one in the halls. The Cobra lived up to his reputation. In the darkened cafeteria, the scent of his clove cigarette filled the air.

His voice poured from the shadows. "That display tonight changes things. We can't wait till next week. We got to move right away."

"Move where?" I said.

"You'll find out soon enough."

Klug stepped into the faint glow from the corridor lights and gestured for me to follow him. He led me through the kitchen to a passage that connected with a hallway to the administrative wing. There I hesitated.

"No one will see us," Klug said. "It's taken care of for an hour at least. No worries. Come on."

We crept across the linoleum floor and ducked inside a stairwell that led up to another level. From there we mounted two more flights of steps and then emerged outdoors atop the wall below one of the guard towers. Two people waited there. One was a guard whose badge read Combest; the other was a nurse from the infirmary, Townsend. I had seen her before but never so close. When the breeze tossed her dark hair, I found myself staring at the curve of her jaw where it sloped down from her ear. In that shadowy light, she looked a lot like Evelyn.

"You're late," said Combest.

"No, we're not," Klug said. "Where are the others?"

Combest indicated the tower and a metal ladder up to the observation deck. We climbed single file. Inside the glass walls of the watch room waited another guard, Mason, and two cons hunkered down out of sight on the floor.

"This him?" said Mason.

"That's him, Mason."

"I read your file, college boy," Mason said. "That pretty face of yours may play with dumb-ass TV reporters and overfed sheeple, but it means nothing in here. If you go grandstanding on us I'll have no hesitation putting a bullet in your head. Understand me?"

"Well," I said, "you can try."

Mason withdrew a step. A flicker of uncertainty lit his eyes.

"No time for this crap, Mason," said Klug. "Cornell's with me. He's one of us. And right now we have business to discuss."

I recognized the two on the floor, Jaime and Scopes, enforcers for Klug. They pulled me down beside them.

"Keep out of sight, asshole," Jaime said.

Klug squatted, too, unfolding a piece of paper from his shirt pocket. He flattened it out on the floor, providing us with a rough map of the prison. He took us step-by-step through the plan. We would leave by the west loading docks, which Grove had sealed up when deliveries stopped arriving. The whole area was shut down, lightly guarded at best, and that would give us a fair chance of slipping away unnoticed. There were three trucks there. Tomorrow night, Combest and a guard named Georges would sneak in, siphon the gas from two of the trucks, and store it all in the third. Meanwhile Townsend would pack medical supplies boosted from the infirmary. Later Combest would meet with Paulson and gather provisions from the kitchen, where Paulson supervised the afternoon work crew. Mason would see to weapons.

We would leave between eleven and midnight, with Klug making arrangements for clear passage from our cells to the loading dock. Money was worthless, but there were other forms of bribery and coercion, and I had no doubt Klug was expert at them all. The last piece fell on Paulson, who sometime in the evening would secure the keys and punch codes for the garage doors and perimeter exits. After that all we had to do was ride, and I got to play navigator.

"We go in two days," said Klug. "Before *Preacher* Grove gets a chance to save our souls for us."

Mason waved me over to the window. "Come here."

I looked out over the north field. Mason switched on a spotlight. The beam slashed the night and illuminated the aimless wormfeeders shuffling along the fence, circling what must have seemed to them a butcher shop late to open for business.

"I know you've been in the hole, so I want to make sure you see what we're up against," Mason said.

"Shut that fucking light off," said Klug. "You'll get us noticed."

"Nobody's gonna notice. Nobody's gonna care. Get bored up here, and it's time for a little target practice. We all do it. Happens every night," Mason said. "Here, look."

He handed me a pair of binoculars.

Except for their decay, the dead things resembled drugged mental patients, empty and tuned into a frequency the living could not hear. Mason hefted his rifle and sighted through the scope. The slug caught one of the corpses in the eye and exploded out the back of its head. The body fell over and rolled around in the dirt, its stained necktie flapping like a tongue.

Mason squeezed off another round, but aimed wide and split the calf of a dead woman passing behind his target, knocking her over. He fired again, taking out necktie's other eye, flattening him to the ground, where he flopped around and tried to get up.

"Doesn't stop them," Mason told me. "They still smell us fine, or sense us, or whatever, but it evens the odds a bit if they can't see to chase us."

I scanned the herd of wormfeeders, seeing many empty eye sockets that had been blown out by rifle fire.

"I wanted you to know I'm a damn good shot," said Mason.

"You missed that second one," I said.

"Think you can do better?"

"Hand me the gun."

"Fuck, no."

"Gonna have to trust me sooner or later."

"Enough," Klug said. "We need to get back now."

I shrugged. What the hell? I'd have my contest with Mason another time. I was sure if we spent any amount of time together—sooner or later—it would come.

Klug and I clambered down the ladder with Jaime and Scopes, quiet as we could. The administration wing stood as empty and still as we'd left it. At the cafeteria, the four of us split to return to our cells. Klug and Scopes headed off into the darkness; Jaime and I moved together toward our cellblock. We didn't speak, but Jaime helped me find my way back along a path different than the one I'd taken to meet Klug. It led to a hallway that connected to the cellblock on the other side of my cell, and that's where they jumped us: two Aryan Brotherhood shitheads, looking for me for payback.

One of them took Jaime off his feet with a pipe to the back of his legs, and the other threw his weight at me, trying to connect with a makeshift sap of rocks stuffed into a rag. He was fat and slow and I dodged every shot, sliding along the floor until his mass shifted enough that I could free my shiv. The fat man dripped sweat and squawked about what he was going to do to me once he made me his punk, how my ass would be his to peddle to all his friends, and his first customer would be Baldwin. Turns out scaredy-cat Baldwin had slipped them as many cigarettes as he could scrounge together to take me out before I killed him. Fat man gave me more than an earful before I thrust the broken penknife blade into his neck and forced it until the tip broke out the back. He cried out and then dropped his dead weight on me like a falling cow.

I fought my way loose from his bulk, figuring his partner would be done with Jaime soon and coming for me. What I found when I crawled out from under, though, was Jaime propped up against the wall, both knees shattered, but the bloodied pipe gripped tight in his hands. Beside him, laid out with a shattered skull, stretched the second skinhead.

"Shit, brother," I said. "Your legs are all fucked up."

"Get out of here," Jaime said, wheezing from pain. "The King Snake's gonna need you. You got maybe four minutes before these fucks get up again. I ain't going anywhere with broken knees, so fucking leave me like you never met me. Go! Now!"

I've never been one to argue with good sense. Jaime was a lost cause as far as escaping and that meant he was as good as dead. It wouldn't do anyone a damn bit of good for me to be found covered in blood and out of my cell after lights out. I wrenched my shiv free from fat man's throat and threw it to Jaime.

"You might need this," I said.

"For them?" Jamie said. "Or for me?"

"Your choice."

I jumped shadows back to my cell. When I got there I pressed a pillow over Baldwin's face without even slowing down and beat him until my knuckles got raw. I made sure he knew how the dogs he'd sicced on me had died and how I held him responsible for losing Jaime. Only thing that kept me from killing him then and there was knowing the son of a bitch wouldn't stay dead.

SEVEN

That night I dreamt of Evelyn rising from her grave, pleading with me to find her, and I tried to, I really did, but the harder I looked, the more she faded away until she vanished altogether. After that I wandered through a field of mist, where foggy gray eddies hid something right beyond my sight. Giant fleeting shapes moved by me and strange masses passed overhead.

Voices called out, speaking names I didn't know. I walked for what felt like hours, lost, aimless, until I tripped over something hard and fell to the ground.

Lying on my back, I looked up and watched the mists peel away. Hundreds of pairs of eyes stared at me through the gray haze. They floated in the gloom, dim constellations of observance, of judgment, all of them focused on me. I covered my face with my hands to blot them out and scrambled to my feet. When I dared to look again, the mist and the eyes were gone. The world revealed was like it always had been, except that everyone was dead and decomposing: grinning corpses drove cars, worked in stores, walked in and out of office buildings. A baby rolled by in a stroller with a bottle of blood clutched in its pudgy gray hands. Its mother smiled as she pushed the stroller around a corner. By the time I realized who they were, they were already gone. I searched for them, but the streets of the city went on forever like a wild maze of hot concrete and shining steel radiating out from me. Alleys became dead ends. Bars appeared in windows. Sidewalks circled back on themselves. The air grew wet and suffocating. I found a deep, empty doorway and sunk into it, pulling out from the flow of dead life that coursed through the streets.

I snapped awake with Evelyn's laughter echoing in my head. Lying in the dark, listening to my memories, thinking of Evelyn and all I'd put behind me and all that lay ahead—that was the first time in my life the notion of suicide ever sprang to mind.

Well, I thought, *fuck that.*

DELLA:
EIGHT

Della Townsend only ever trusted two men in her life and both had died long before the dead plague began. No matter how much she missed them, she was grateful her brother and her father had not lived to see what became of the world. Six months back Della had lost her mother, too, and she had thought she could not get any more alone than that. Life had proven her wrong when it stranded her, one of three women trapped in a prison full of violent men under siege by the walking dead. It did not matter that Warden Grove gave the women secure, private quarters and declared them off limits to protect their so-called virtue. His word was insufficient to stop the propositions and insinuations, the leers, and crude gestures, and the surreptitious gropes whenever an opportunity presented itself. That Della did not get along with the other nurses—Lucinda Tancredo and Sue Oberon—was no help to her situation either. Lucinda and Sue were young and naive enough to believe the dead plague would blow over and pretty soon life would go back to normal.

They flirted with the guards. To get things they wanted and make sure they had protectors, they even fucked some of them, taking care to keep it secret from the warden. Della did not do such things. She worked in the infirmary, sometimes sixteen hours a day, and when she was not working, she kept herself closed off in the cell she had been given as living quarters. Not a man inside failed to remind her in some way of her two ex-husbands, and those men had taught her more than a few hard lessons. She knew it was inevitable, though, that men would come for her, probably two or three at once to make sure she could not resist. She had already broken the nose of one guard who had grabbed her ass and smacked another who had propositioned her, and she had even seen a strange light in Warden Grove's eyes when he looked at her the last time he visited the infirmary. She knew men like this resented her for holding back. Sooner or later, they would want to put her in her place. She hoped she would be long gone before that happened.

If she really needed help, there was Combest. He liked to come by her cell, tapping his club against the bars, smiling while he waited for her to invite him in, like he was doing now. She nodded for him to enter because it was easier than running him off. She thought she knew what Combest wanted, but he was too soft to take it from her. Still, she sat up straight and smoothed her skirt down to cover her thighs. No reason to encourage him.

"What do you want, Randy?" she said.

"Came to see how you're doing with everything we got going on. Things got a little tense in the tower last night. Thought you might be nervous. Thought we could talk some."

"All right, have a seat."

Della kept a folding chair in her cell, and Combest liked to settle into it like it was made of glass. He set his hands on his knees. They were trembling.

"Think we can do this?" he said.

"We have to, unless you prefer hanging."

"Maybe there's another way. Behind closed doors, Grove's talking like there's going to be something after all this. He's asking some of the guards to delay their salvation so they can help him do God's work later on."

"He ask you?"

"Not yet."

"Not ever. You're not the missionary kind."

Combest tilted his chair back on two legs and balanced there with his head touching the cement wall behind him. He always sat like that, like a submissive dog on its back.

"Bet he asks you."

Della scowled. "I'm not the missionary kind, either."

"Tell you what, though, to his eyes, you're more pure than Lucy and Sue. He knows they're catting around. Doesn't like it, but he figures it cuts the tension among the guards if some of them get a little release now and then. Makes those gals tainted, though. You, on the other hand, he considers a real woman, mature. He has moments when he stares out his office window, pining over his lost Missus, and I swear he's got you on his mind too. Wants you to be the good woman behind the great man."

"I'd just wind up stabbing him in the back. He's cracked. I don't want any part of his work." Della glanced at her watch. Almost 8 a.m. She was due at the infirmary soon.

"You might change your mind if he asks you."

"Not likely. What do you care anyway?"

Combest shrugged. "Figured if you had his ear, you might put in a good word for me."

"You backing out of Klug's plan?"

"No. But I wonder if it's smart. I really want to know: Do you think we can do this thing?"

Della nodded.

"Not sure I trust the King Snake," said Combest.

"Don't. Not even a little. But if anyone can get us out of here, he can. Once we're out, though, watch your back, and be ready for a double-cross."

"I don't like working with cons, especially Klug's thugs, and this new guy, Cornell. Some of the guards aren't much better."

"Mason's solid," Della said. "I knew him a little back in high school. He played football. He was a family man."

"Not anymore."

"No."

"Sad thing, that."

"We're living in sad times."

Combest stood and folded the chair. "I'd feel a lot better if I could get a beer. Used to head home from here at the end of the day, fire up the charcoal grill in the yard, and sit out there with a cold one until sunset. Maybe listen to a little music, or maybe only to the breeze rustling the trees. On Fridays, I'd have a couple of the neighbors over. Sure took the edge off things."

That day, watching Combest fold the chair and lean it against the wall, Della saw him in a different light. He always left her cell with a longing look in his eyes, and she often pitied him for it, thinking it spoke of a base desire, but today it made her wonder what kind of man he had been in the old world. Maybe she had read him wrong. Maybe he was not after her, but only looking for a neighbor to talk to and a normal conversation to make life seem a little less insane.

"What kind of music?" she asked.

"Blues." Combest laughed. "Cause, you know, I thought life was hard back then."

"Randy, did you have family out there?"

Combest straightened, keeping his back to Della. He did not answer her right away. He seemed so still that she felt a twinge of guilt over maybe touching a raw nerve.

"Everybody had family out there," he said. "Everybody has someone."

He moved toward the door, keeping his face turned away, and left. As Combest's footsteps diminished along the corridor, Della thought, *everybody but me.* Then she stood and readied herself for work.

NINE

The dead and dying came in all day that day. A nasty flu had been going around, and there was no medicine to fight it. Most with the virus recovered after a few days; some did not. People whose bodies had not yet picked a side filled the beds. Doctor Foley hardly had any regular patients to treat anymore. He bitched about his infirmary having been turned into a disassembly line, his examination tables into chopping blocks. He could take apart a body in under two minutes if he wanted to, but when the fourth corpse rolled in before noon that day, he started playing a game, using every last second, timing his final snip of the spinal cord with the moment when the dead man's eyes flashed open and his jaw began to click. Foley's game spooked the guards on duty, Calderon and Hammond, as well as Sue Oberon, and it frightened Della. It was not the risk that bothered her so much as it was the change in Foley's demeanor. He declined her offer to take over for a while so Della let it go and kept working until her white dress was stained almost solid red.

Every chance she got, she slipped a few more items out of the medicine cabinet and hid them in her clothes. The cabinet should have been locked, but Foley was too distracted or too tired to care about such details. She had already collected antibiotics, sterile gauze and bandages, analgesics, surgical thread and needles, and a thermometer, and she planned to lift more things later. She wanted to take some morphine and Valium, but those supplies were running low, so she would have to wait until the last opportunity or their absence would be noticed. Mason, the third guard working chop duty that day, ran interference, distracting the others and blocking Della from sight whenever he could. Of all the men trapped in the prison, Mason was the only one Della liked, but he was so immersed in anger and grief, she thought it might end him.

Mason went off duty at 4 p.m., and by then, Della had doubled the supplies she had already lifted. The stream of incoming dead dried up, although more would no doubt come later. Tancredo and Oberon left for the cafeteria, and Foley went into his office to nap and closed the door, leaving Della and

Mason alone in the gore-stained room. Della took cleaning supplies out of a closet, set them on a countertop, and prepared to scrub. She saw Mason heading for the door and caught him by the arm on his way out.

"Hey," she whispered. "Thanks. Got us a good stash going."

"We'll need it," Mason said.

"I want to ask you something," she said. "Why don't you ever talk about it?"

"About what?"

"The day the bus came. If I were you I'd have died that day."

"Dying doesn't mean what it used to."

"You know what I mean." Della let go of Mason's arm and then lifted two bottles of ammonia from the mop bucket. "You ever want to talk it out, I'm here. Okay?"

"Tell me something. You hear a lot of guards talking about who they lost? About their families, wives, girlfriends?"

"Not too many."

"Because they don't know what happened to them, and long as it stays that way, maybe what's keeping them going is hoping that *their* family, *their* wife, *their* girlfriend got lucky, that someone who loves them is hiding someplace safe, waiting for them to come home. Me, *I know*. I saw them at the end, standing proud and beautiful while that insane, self-righteous shitsmear had them murdered in front of me."

Della felt foolish and clumsy. She did not comprehend the depth of bitterness and grief in Mason's voice. It was like a deep vein of toxic metal running through the earth.

"You remember what Grove said when it happened?" Mason asked.

Della had rushed up to the tower with Doctor Foley that day to argue that if Grove would not let the people on the bus into the prison then he should at least allow Foley out to treat their injured. Grove hadn't even let Foley speak. He had been preoccupied with Mason, who had gotten there first to plead for the lives of his family. The warden ranted like a true fire-and-brimstone preacher, but she could not recall what he had said. Too many people had been shouting. She shook her head.

"I remember. He said, 'There's the world out there, and it has its sinners, and here inside these walls, we have ours. For now the world out there is dead to us. That's God's plan. You and I aren't to question it,'" Mason said. "Then he gave the order to open fire."

Della remembered Mason screaming after that, almost as loud as the gunfire, his voice echoing in the watchtower.

"Don't know how much you saw then or if you knew who was who. My boys survived the gunfire. My wife didn't. The dead got up and finished off the wounded."

"I'm sorry," Della said. "I...I shouldn't have asked."

"S'all right. I know you meant well," Mason said. "I'm coping as well as any man could. Okay? So don't fret about me cracking when we bust out of here."

"I won't. I wasn't."

"The thing I can't stop thinking about is how Melissa and the boys must have felt so relieved when they reached the prison, thinking they'd found sanctuary, only to have it yanked away from them. Every time I close my eyes, I see her, how she stood with my sons, while all the people from the bus pounded on the gates. She knew I was watching, and she wouldn't cry or show fear. Maybe she believed I'd find a way to come through and get them inside. Whatever they'd done to make it this far, whatever they'd suffered, they'd only fought for a chance that never existed. I won't be surprised once we leave this place, if we find ourselves in the same position."

"Mason." Della placed her hand on his arm.

"You know when it was all over that bastard Grove had the nerve to say a prayer for them?"

Della remembered that part. It had sent Mason into such a violent rage that the other guards had cuffed him and dragged him into a cell to cool down.

"I keep my mouth shut," Mason said, "Because I don't want to take anyone else's hope away. In a perverse way, I'm one of the lucky ones. The wondering is over for me. I know. *I. Know.* I owe that to Warden Grove. So, if you think you're going to cozy up and comfort me, and we're going to bust out of this place running together for some happy ending, you'll be a lot better off sticking to your bandages and your medicine."

Mason shook free of Della's hand and left.

Della sank to a chair and cried.

When she looked up again, Foley stood in the open door of his office, staring at her with wet, bloodshot eyes. He was looking at her hip. Della glanced at what had caught his eye. One of her lab coat pockets had split, and a wad of antibiotics packets was poking out.

"Shit," she said.

TEN

"Don't think I don't know what you're planning." Foley closed his office door behind him and Della. "I don't know the details, but a breakout is a breakout, and I understand now more than ever why people want out of here. Hell, a few weeks ago, I might've asked to come with you. So keep taking what you need on the sly, and I'll keep pretending I don't notice the missing inventory and how things have been rearranged on the shelf to make it look like there's more than there is. That isn't why I wanted to talk to you."

"No?" Della said.

Foley opened a drawer in his desk, removed a bottle of scotch, and set it on the blotter in front of him. It looked like smoky gold. He placed a paper cup beside it then filled the cup and offered it to Della. It surprised him when she accepted it. He produced another paper cup and poured a drink for himself.

"Bottoms up," he said.

Foley and Della drank. The doctor refilled their cups then put the bottle away.

"Sip this one," he said. "Don't know where or when I'll ever find more."

Della studied Foley's tired eyes. She knew he had become jaded—that had been inevitable—but she still saw a spark there of the compassionate, intelligent man she had met when she first started working with him. She had recommended to Klug that they include Foley in the breakout, but Klug had rejected him. Too independent, too high minded, too likely to be a problem, he had said, and she could not persuade him.

"If you're lighting out for the territories," Foley said, "there's some information you really ought to have."

"Like what?"

Foley hesitated. He looked Della up and down, and for half a moment, she feared he was going to proposition her or try to blackmail her for sex. Instead, he only nodded to himself as if he had answered an unspoken question. Then he reached under his desk and produced a black briefcase. He opened it and removed a case-hardened laptop. Della felt a gasp of air pass between her lips.

"You know you can't tell anyone I have this, right?" Foley said.

"I know," Della said. "Grove would punish you. Not that it's worth a damn since the 'Net went down."

"This one happens to be worth far more than a damn," Foley said. "The truth is, the 'Net may be down, but it isn't dead and buried yet."

He typed on the laptop keyboard then swiveled it around to show Della the screen. A Web browser displayed a grid of thumbnail images, links to videos, photo galleries, and documents.

"What the hell?" Della said.

"Don't get too excited. The public 'Net is gone. This one will be too soon. But for now it's still cooking, although there's nobody minding the shop. Doesn't matter. Very few people can access it. You need government or military clearance, an encrypted satellite connection, and last but not least, one of these spiffy combat-grade laptops."

"Why do you have that?"

"Got it from the CDC," Foley said. "I never meant to make a career out of being a prison doctor. I was on track for a research post in Atlanta, as of eight months ago. The Army drafted me for a little advance field work. Hooked me up with this. Had me filing data based on my observations here. They were interested in everything from basic vitals to illness trends to psychological conditions. Never told me why. I didn't ask. That comes with the job I'd applied for, so I think this was something of a trial run. But none of that's important. Look here."

Foley moved the cursor over a grainy thumbnail and clicked the link. A video player replaced the grid. A fuzzy image filled its screen. Beneath the image were the words "Posted by Birch," followed by a date from last week. Foley clicked play. The image sprang to jerking motion. A pair of eyes peered out from rotted flesh. The focus was poor, but the eyes swiveling in their sockets were vibrant and white. They glistened. Della did not understand. She glanced at Foley, who directed her back to the screen. The movie focus blurred then sharpened and the view inched back. The eyes diminished in the frame. The skin around them shifted and wrinkled. Movement came into the top of the frame. It took Della several seconds to realize what she was looking at. It was a dead man restrained in chains, facing away from the camera, and snarling as he tried to look over his shoulder. The eyes at the center of the image were embedded in his back, below the base of his neck. The video ended and froze on the same image with which it had started.

"What...?" Della said. "What is that?"

"Damned if I know," said Foley. "But it's something real. I know Birch. He's a doctor and a military officer. I've traded a few e-mails with him, but he's finicky about keeping in touch. Remember when this all started and we figured somewhere someone was holed up working out a solution? That's Birch. The punch-line is he's stumped. But he's gone further than anyone else trying to decipher this nightmare. So when he posted this, I...well, I didn't know what to think. I've seen this twice in the last few days. An eyeball where it shouldn't be. In someone's foot the first time. In a kidney the second. I figured it was some anomaly, tissue growing where it shouldn't, like cancer, but tissue shouldn't be growing at all in the dead. I don't want people asking me any more questions I can't hope to answer so I kept it quiet."

"Why are you telling me?"

Foley closed the laptop, slipped it back into its case, and stuck it under his desk. "You're going out there. You need to be prepared. You need to know."

"That the dead have eyeballs in strange places?"

Foley shook his head. "That the dead are changing."

CORNELL:
ELEVEN

Figured I was done for the next morning when the screws caught sight of beaten and bruised Baldwin, but he covered up best he could, hid the limp I'd given him, and said nothing. He'd had one shot in him and it had failed. That sad son of a bitch would've eaten glass and stuck his hand in a blender if I told him to after that.

Gave me a scare, though, when the screws fetched me away from breakfast for an audience with Warden Grove. Two of them brought me to the administration wing and planted me on a bench outside the warden's office. After awhile another con came out, blubbering like a baby, eyes swollen, face red and purple. He clutched his left arm against his chest as he stumbled off in the direction of the infirmary.

My turn next.

Standard procedure for an audience with Grove meant standing stiff-backed and motionless in the warden's office while he reclined in a leather chair, puffing on a cigar, and two guards stood watch. Today it was Gamewood and Hammond. They ushered me in and Grove made me wait a little longer while he stared me down. Behind him a window looked out over the south lawn, where the road to town cut a dusty scar through the fields. Wormfeeders dotted the grass like a herd of strange livestock.

"Good morning, Mr. Cornell," Grove said. "Good of you to take the time to see me."

"Yes, sir."

Grove blew a cloud of smoke toward me. It drifted up and across the room's sparse decoration—a wall of framed photographs of the warden from his days as a preacher, stumping at the pulpit, shaking hands with local bigwigs and state politicians. He had a few diplomas mixed in, and here and there pictures of his family. I wondered how he felt about losing them. Probably pleased as fucking punch that they were united with God and looking forward to joining them.

"After a good many years preaching, I felt the need for a new challenge," he told me, noticing my interest. "Ten years ago I came here to shine the light of truth on the wicked. It has been most rewarding. Now, you may be wondering what this has to do with you. Well, given recent events, it seemed appropriate you should have the same chance for salvation as any other man in my keep. I let you witness my good works in the yard, and I hoped you would be swayed by them."

Grove took a thick file from his drawer and dropped it on his desk blotter. He opened it and leafed through a stack of clippings and photocopies covering my story.

"Then I realized that I was mistaken. You're a different kind of man than most incarcerated here. Your road to redemption cannot be as simple as theirs. You're an intelligent, capable fellow, Mr. Cornell. But I believe you're crippled by a towering sadness."

He lifted a scrap of newspaper with a photo of Evelyn. The picture had been in a camera I had when the police arrested me, but Evelyn had been dead by the time it was published.

"Could I be correct?" Grove said.

The warden was good, I'll grant him. He sniffed out my weak spot like a crow digging for grubs. I didn't answer.

"Tell me about her," he said.

"Nothing to tell anymore."

"Did you love her? She was with child when she died, wasn't she? Was it yours? A new life. Were you happy about that or did it terrify you? Maybe both?"

"I don't want to talk about it."

Grove snapped his fingers. Gamewood slammed his club into my kidney. The pain buckled me to my knees. I clenched my teeth against a scream.

"I'm a patient, understanding man," said Grove. "Share your grief with me. Share it with the Lord. Let go your burden and cleanse yourself."

Gamewood struck again, glancing his wood off my shoulder blade. Fresh hurt blasted through me like slivers of hot glass.

"The way to redemption begins with the admission of sin," Grove said. "Do you hate yourself for leading your woman to a wretched life that got her killed?"

Despite my throbbing aches, I laughed. No one had ever led Evelyn to do anything.

"No? The child, then? Help me out here, Mr. Cornell. We both know you don't lose any sleep over the money you stole. That was only ever a means for you, not an end. Such pedestrian transgressions are of little interest to either one of us, I think."

Hammond's boot slammed my stomach, lifted me onto my side, and left me gasping for air.

"Whether you know it or not, choose to accept it or deny it, you've arrived at a crossroads. Your body will die and rot, as all men's bodies do. The question is whether your soul will remain trapped within it after your death or be freed to obtain its heavenly reward. I offer you salvation, Mr. Cornell. You suffer no easy pain, but time heals all wounds. I can give you the opportunity to lick yours and knit your soul back together."

A fist crushed the back of my neck and drove me to the floor. I smacked my forehead, bit my tongue, and saw stars.

"You're a charming, gifted young man with the ability to secure people's loyalty and capture their imagination as well as demand their attention and obedience. These are skills I'd find most useful in my upcoming mission. My work here will end soon. Last night commenced the final stage. Those who can be saved here will be, and those who cannot be saved will be sent to their eternal damnation. When that is done, I'll lead a group of men into the world to free those worthy of redemption and guide any we might find still living toward their everlasting rewards. There are many, many good souls trapped in foul decaying flesh. God has charged me with their rescue."

I clawed onto all fours, only to feel Gamewood's baton lash into my thigh. It knocked me sideways, and I gasped.

"You possess the elements of a leader. With your charisma you could have been a businessman, an entertainer, even a politician. But life dealt you a bad hand, didn't it?" Grove skimmed pages in his file and pulled out a copy of an old police report. "A good student with and aptitude for language and science, until at age 17, you were arrested for armed robbery, carrying a busted gun that couldn't even be fired. Bet you got a story to tell about that. Your two friends took pleas, fingered you as the ringleader, and did eighteen months in juvenile detention. You took your chances with a jury and wound up sentenced as an adult. Served nine years. I imagine you learned an awful lot about robbing banks in that time, and maybe made a few useful connections."

Grove stacked the papers and closed the folder.

"There's something better than that inside you. You need some time to find it and let it out. Why not do some good while you get your soul right? A man like you could help sustain my men's commitment and help me win the trust of the wanting multitudes."

My thoughts whirled like mud in a rain-swept river. Pain rose in me like floodwaters. I clung to a flotsam desire to lighten the burden I'd borne since the day Evelyn died and part of me began to buy into Grove's insanity. He was right about one thing: I needed to face my guilt for letting down Evelyn, for betraying us both through my failure. I'd fooled myself long enough about that. I could never straighten myself out in prison, cowering and scraping to survive when I should be running circles around these madmen and losers. "Play by your own rules," Evelyn had always said, but I'd given up. I'd forgotten and hobbled myself, thereby making my debt to her a thousand times worse.

Grove offered a way out—except I already had that, I reminded myself, unless I get beaten so badly I can't walk. Like Jaime. Then that door shuts forever.

"Evelyn..." I said, gasping for air. "I promised Evelyn...two things. Protect her always...and never...kill a man...in cold blood. Broke both...the day she died."

It was the truth. Grove would've known if it wasn't. But speaking those few words hurt more than any beating ever could. I had fired on the bank manager in a blistering rage after he shot Evelyn, but those two rent-a-cops had been as shocked as I was when their boss drew his weapon. They would've backed down. I didn't need to kill them. I wanted to do it because all the light had left my world and cast me in such despair that killing seemed like no big thing when in fact it was of such a magnitude that it threatened to overwhelm and obliterate me even now. That's how the jackal snares its prey; it waits for that solitary error, that wrong turn from which there's no recovering.

"Thank you." Grove waved off the guards. "I appreciate your honesty."

He circled his desk, lifted me under the arms, and helped me to a chair. He took a handkerchief from his pocket, wiped the blood from my face, and left the cloth in my hand. He poured a glass of water and held it to my lips so I could sip from it. Every inch the Good Samaritan.

"Who decides?" Needles of pain flared behind my eyes. Blood oozed down the back of my throat. "Who says...who's worth saving...and who gets damned?"

"God has appointed that burden to me." Grove's quiet, unbreakable voice made me feel like worms were eating their way out of my stomach. "I'm here to do His work, and I shall not flinch from my duties."

"When you're done?"

"We all go to our reward someday."

It's only another way out, I told myself. That's all. A back-up plan. Make no more of it. Break out with Klug or throw in with this lunatic, once I'm on the other side of the walls, I can get away clean, no problem. Sometimes it's okay to play by the crazy man's rules, long as you don't forget your own.

"You'll begin your mission tonight. You'll assist me at the gallows. The men have heard the Word from me too often. They resent it. A new voice must deliver them the message of salvation. It has to come from one of their own, now," Grove said.

I hadn't anticipated that.

Damn jackal had pounced when I was down, and his hot breath was steaming at the back of my neck.

TWELVE

Things didn't go well for Jaime.

The guards found him fighting off the resurrected skinheads with my shiv in time to keep him alive, but his blood drove one of the bastards to gnaw clean through his leg above the knee. Damn shame a right guy who could fight like that losing a leg. Least he didn't have to live with it long.

That night he came propped up on crutches with the first group of penitent convicts Warden Gove paraded onto the gallows. Jaime played along with Grove's theatrics. When the executioner fitted his hood, he welcomed it with an oddly gratified expression, like he'd finally gotten the answer to some question that had been itching away under his skin for a long time. I saw it because I was standing three feet to his right. Then the traps opened, and Jaime and his two companions dropped into oblivion. Grove let them hang a while, before the hacks untied them and threw their quaking bodies on the bonfire.

Better than spending your last days a cripple lying around waiting for the end, I suppose.

Others had the same idea. The beaten man who'd passed me outside the warden's office that morning was in the next trio, with his busted arm in a sling. Some of the cons had bought into Grove's proposition, and the warden couldn't have looked more pleased with how it was going. But every time he flashed his swinish grin, I thought of Combest and Georges, who were right at that moment siphoning gas in the loading dock. By the end of the day tomorrow, Warden Grove would be another bad memory in the back of my mind.

Midway through the service Grove had the guards usher me to center stage, where I spouted the words Grove had scripted, mixing them up like he'd asked to make them sound like my own. When you rob banks for a living, you become attuned to the sensation of having people's attention, and I had plenty of it that night in the form of seething hatred and unfettered disgust from the convicts who thought I'd flipped to save my own skin. Guess they were right, even if the words meant nothing to me. But I didn't care what they thought. There was no reason for me to play it their way and wind up dead. Them judging me made them no different than all the other people I'd known wanting to tell me how I ought to live and resenting me for not buying their bullshit code. That night I saw no difference between my fellow inmates and the men who'd locked us all away, or even the hungry, mindless dead. Shit, at least the goddamned wormfeeders didn't lie about wanting to eat you.

After my speech, three cons took the platform. They were different than the others. They'd been beaten and crushed, all right, but anger still smoldered in their expressions. If they could've gotten loose, they'd have torn me and Grove and everyone else on the platform limb from limb. The supercops had to drag them out in cuffs and hold them tight while they roped them up. Grove kept right on preaching.

"Words do not allow me to adequately express how pleased I am that some of you have chosen to accept my aid in securing eternal salvation. I have faith that more will make the same decision. But I understand that some among you are incorrigible and incapable of repenting your ways, and I have elected to waste no time with men of such disposition, men like this trio of unrepentant sinners behind me. Witness their fate. It is the end of all those who choose the path of sin over forgiveness. May they do some good by their example."

The hatches popped open and the men dropped through. I felt a genuine pang of loss watching those unbroken spirits die. Felt a little sick when their corpses began to twitch around at the end of their ropes. Grove left them there for a time, making us all watch, and then the screws came, hauled them up, and dragged them away. It was not to the bonfire they took them but to a steel pen erected beside the gallows to Grove's left-hand side. In they went, tumbling over each other as they clambered onto their feet. They reached through the bars, straining toward the crowd, their heads tilted at strange angles on noose-snapped necks. They couldn't see through their hoods, but there's no doubt they still knew we were there. No doubt at all about their hunger.

THIRTEEN

Next day came the day of the four suicides, and my sudden yearning to return to solitary. Watching that wiry kid burn I suffered my first real pangs of doubt about our chances. I shrugged them off, though, and took heart in how all that hubbub made a fine distraction for Paulson and Combest sneaking provisions from the kitchen and Della slipping medical supplies out of the infirmary. That afternoon I crossed paths with the King Snake in the yard.

"Don't cross me, Cornell," he said. "Your song and dance for Grove better be nothing more than an act."

"Do I strike you as the preaching type?"

"Heh. No," Klug said.

"Grove dragged me into his office and gave me an ultimatum. Had a couple of hacks sweet talk me with batons, too, as you might have noticed," I said. "This shit is only me going along to buy time."

"I know all about it. You did what you had to. Kept your mouth shut, too. Okay. Right now I still trust you. So you keep doing what you have to. Word is out you're still under my protection no matter what your fellow inmates would like to do to you for turning Judas on them. So, stay tight with Grove for now. Just makes it all the sweeter when we pull this off right under his nose. But if you try to fuck with me, I will turn your skull into my personal piss pot."

Klug moved on before I could answer, not wanting to be seen talking to me too long. He never mentioned Jaime.

DELLA:
FOURTEEN

The afternoon before the breakout, blood coated almost every surface in the infirmary. No one bothered cleaning up right away, especially after the run of corpses that had come in that morning and afternoon. Fights were breaking out every few hours, now, and more than a few of them resulted in at least one fatality. Everyone knew there would simply be more dead later or tomorrow or the next day, until Warden Grove finished his work or the last shred of order broke down inside the prison and the bodies lay where they fell until they got up again. Rumors were some of the gangs were planning mass killings of rivals to throw the prison into chaos so they could seize control. Grove had clamped down so tight, though, that no more than fifty inmates were out of their cells at any one time during the day. As Della watched Calderon and Gamewood cart away the latest pile of bagged, twitching body parts, she hoped everything would hold together for one more night. She did not know how many more bodies she could stand to cut apart. She was almost as fast as Foley, now, but she lacked his detachment. It still hit her hard doing it every day. Foley moved like a machine and between corpses he shut himself off in his office, leaving Della and the other nurses to treat the few cons and guards who came in with everyday ailments.

Late that afternoon the hacks brought in three inmates and a guard, all dead in the wake of a spontaneous suicide in the cafeteria. At the sound of the commotion, Foley shuffled out of his office.

"Only four?" he said. "Piece of cake. Everyone take a body and start carving."

Della, Tancredo, and Foley grabbed tools and moved to work on the dead cons. All of them stopped short when Sue Oberon screamed. She had gone to work on the guard, Phil Hammond. Her knees bent, and she fell against the stainless steel table that held Hammond's corpse. She buried her face against his chest and screamed into it. Clothing and dead flesh muffled her voice.

"We don't have time for this," said Foley. He glanced at the clock as he took Oberon by the shoulders and drew her away from the dead body. "There's nothing you can do now, Sue. Sit this one out, okay? Give me a few minutes, and then I'll get you something to take the edge off."

Oberon erupted with a shout and twisted away, shoving Foley aside. She grabbed a scalpel from a tray of surgical tools and waved it in front of her. "Don't you fucking touch me! Don't anybody touch me. And nobody touches Phil."

"Sue, please," Della said. "He's gone, honey. I know how you felt about him, but the man you knew is dead. And you know what he's going to be when he comes back."

"I don't care." Oberon backed up against Hammond's table and grabbed his pale hand. "It's not right. It shouldn't be him, not Phil. We were going to stay together when all this bullshit blew over. We were going to be together outside."

"That was never going to happen, Sue," Foley said. "This won't ever blow over. The dead plague isn't going away, but if you don't put down the scalpel and let us do our jobs, you, me, and everyone in this room stands a good chance of winding up like Phil right now, today."

"Go ahead. Do what you want to the others. No one touches Phil," Oberon said.

Foley sighed. "All right people, watch the clock. Della, Lucinda, start on the others. Gamewood and Calderon, grab blades and start cutting."

"Fuck that, I don't know what to do," said Calderon.

"It's not surgery, Raul. Just slice them apart," Foley said. "Work fast. Immobilize them. Sever the joints."

The clock over the door loomed like the noonday sun. Beneath its steady ticking, the nurses and guards became blurs of motion, blood-smeared uniforms tipped with surgical steel edges that bit into cooling flesh.

Foley approached Oberon. "Sue, drop the blade now. You're a good nurse. I can't afford to lose you."

"Fuck you. Stay away."

"Please, Sue."

"No," she said. Her voice lowered to almost a whimper. "Maybe...maybe Phil will be different when he rises."

"He won't be," Foley said.

"You don't know for sure. You can't know."

"Don't be childish. It's not like Hammond was your only boyfriend. Everyone knows how you are. Someone else will take his place inside of a week, and you'll forget all about Hammond. You're in shock now. Put it in perspective. He didn't really matter to you that much, did he? He gave you nothing you won't be able to get from the next man in line you let into your bed."

Oberon gaped as if she had been slapped.

Della cringed at the cruelty of Foley's words, but sometimes that was what it took to reach people who were not thinking straight. Oberon wavered. Her hand holding the scalpel dipped. Tears streamed from her eyes. Foley edged closer. Della released the deep breath she had been holding, but then the hand she was cutting away from its wrist jerked to life and its clumsy fingers grabbed at her. Too much time had passed.

A moment later, Hammond's corpse jerked sideways, dropped halfway off the table, and grabbed onto Oberon as it slid the rest of the way over the edge. The dead thing pulled the nurse to the floor with it. Oberon screamed, the sadness in her voice replaced with terror. Foley rushed forward, grabbed Oberon's arms, braced his foot against Hammond's dripping torso, and tried to pull them apart. The dead man sank his teeth into the nurse's back and clamped down. Oberon flailed as Hammond's mouth ground down to her bone. She panicked and slashed the scalpel, slicing Foley's arm. The doctor swore and jumped away. Blood welled up along a six-inch gash down his sleeve.

"A little help?" Foley said.

Calderon and Gamewood had cut every joint on one dead con and were helping Tancredo finish off another. Della worked on the third with a cut through the neck and spine. All three dead men bucked on their tables, broken bodies drawn toward the living flesh beyond their reach. Della darted across the room and grabbed Foley, shoving his sleeve up to examine his cut. It was clean and shallow but bleeding fast. She pulled adhesive pressure bandages from the cabinet and began slapping them on in a row up Foley's arm like giant stitches.

Calderon shouted and swung a motorized surgical saw, aiming for Hammond's neck. Gamewood came from the other side with an electric bone saw and pressed the whirling blade into the dead guard's shoulder. The saws cut flesh and sent blood spurting onto Oberon, starting her screaming again.

"Somebody get her clear," Gamewood said.

Tancredo grabbed her friend's arm and tried to pull her loose, but Oberon sagged, dead weight. Her eyes blanked out. Calderon wrenched his saw free and swung again, trying to sever Hammond's neck, but the dead man lurched sideways and the saw blade punched against Oberon's skull, biting through bone and deep into her head. Tancredo screamed and scrambled away.

"Oh, shit," said Calderon.

Foley pushed past Della and shoved the stunned Calderon aside. He pulled the saw out of Oberon's skull, drawing soft flecks of brain and blood-matted hair with it. Grabbing Hammond's head with one hand, he sawed at the neck with the other.

"It's a saw you fucking imbecile. Not a machete," Foley told Calderon. "What are you so afraid of? How's he going to bite you with his teeth buried in Sue's back? It's a wonder someone as stupid as you remembers to breathe."

Foley drew the saw back and forth twice more; Hammond's head popped loose from its body. Foley yanked it free from Oberon's back, tearing out a chunk of flesh with it. He hurled the head into a corner. Gamewood had severed one of Hammond's arms and now he started on the other. Foley turned to the legs. A minute later, Hammond's corpse lay in pieces on the blood-slicked floor. The room quieted, and the only sounds came from the corpses rattling the tables and Oberon's shallow gasping. She was deep in shock, and she had lost a lot of blood. Tancredo knelt and cradled Oberon's head in her lap.

"Let's finish up here, folks," said Foley. "Clear out the dead. We've got more work ahead of us. Sue's not going to pull through, in case any of you were wondering." Foley was right. Oberon lingered for fifteen minutes, during which time Della and Foley worked with Calderon and Gamewood to bag and dump the four corpses they had cut to pieces. Tancredo stayed with Oberon, waiting until she breathed her last, and then she called Foley. The doctor declared her time of death, and with help from Gamewood, lifted her body onto a table. He took Oberon apart with unexpected gentleness. No one spoke. Everyone wanted her bagged and dumped before she started twitching. No one wanted to watch her resurrection. They almost made it.

Afterward Foley looked at Della with a wild gaze. "Getting out of here is a damn fine idea," he whispered to her. Then he went in his office and shut the door.

FIFTEEN

Having lost a guard and a nurse from his staff, Warden Grove came to visit the infirmary. He surveyed the gore and bits of dead flesh everywhere, looked at the damage done to the cabinets and tables, and shuddered at the sight of Gamewood and Della, both painted nearly black with drying streaks of blood. He bowed his head and prayed. His lips moved soundlessly for several minutes. He looked humbled. Della stopped mopping and waited in silence until he finished his prayer.

Grove lifted his head. "Where are the others?"

"Calderon went to change his uniform. Tancredo walked out. Don't know where to," said Gamewood.

"She and Sue were close," Della said. "Sue died in her arms."

"Doctor Foley?"

"Resting in his office." Gamewood gestured at the door.

"I'll get to him in a minute, then. Tell me how it happened," Grove said.

"Yeah, the kitchen crew brought in four bodies," said Gamewood, but he stopped when the warden waved him silent.

"Your story I'll read in your report, Mr. Gamewood." Grove took the mop from Della's hands and placed it in the bucket. "Are you injured?"

"No," Della said.

"That's good. Would you tell me what happened? Are you all right to talk about it?"

"It's like he said, they brought in four dead," said Della. She leaned back against the countertop and explained to Grove how Sue's reaction had endangered them all and led to her death.

"The wages of sin," Grove said when Della finished. "And incompetence, from the sound of it. Consider Calderon permanently off chop duty. I'll find him something equally unpleasant but better suited to his poor skills. Thank the Lord no one else was hurt."

Grove's gaze made a circuit of the room as if he were searching for something or cataloging the ruin. The rotten aroma of dead flesh and eviscerated bodies filled the air. It was like the constant taint of decay that hung in the atmosphere but a thousand times more potent.

"This is no place for a woman," Grove said. "Bless you for the good work you do, Ms. Townsend."

Della stiffened. "Thank you."

"God willing, you won't have to do it much longer. I'm confident the Lord above has other plans for someone as strong as you."

"I wouldn't pretend to know what the Lord has planned."

"It's true, his ways are hard to know, but the death and suffering that fills our days has sharpened my senses. I feel closer to God now than I have in years. He's shown me that I have a road to follow beyond these stone walls and iron bars. There's work for me in the outside world. God has entrusted me with a sacred duty. Thankfully, it isn't one I must undertake alone. I'll have a chosen group to share my burden. I want you to be a part of it. My work here will be finished soon. Then it'll be time for me and a few others to leave. I'd like you to be at my side, not just as a nurse, but as a friend, a colleague, and maybe, given time, something more."

Della slid along the counter away from the warden. She bumped the mop handle and spilled the bucket in which the mop stood. Bloody cleaning fluid gushed onto the tile. Della snatched up the mop and used it to keep the water and detergent from spreading too thin. The soap and bleach cut streaks of clean floor through the blood. Della pushed the mop around, concentrating on the floor to avoid the warden's stare.

"Give it some thought," Grove said. "I'm not asking a small favor. It's a true commitment to me, to the Lord, and to His work. But make sure you consider your options before you answer. You might find them less appealing than a life of righteous service."

Grove crossed the room and knocked on Doctor Foley's door. "Doctor Foley, open up," he said. "It's Warden Grove. Let's talk, son." Foley didn't answer. Grove turned the knob, and shouted, "Wake up, Doctor."

The door cracked open. Grove pushed it inward and leaned into the opening. A hand jutted out and seized him by the hair, tugging hard enough to pull him off balance and send him tumbling to the floor. Foley lurched into view, stumbling over Grove. The doctor's face looked ashen and flaccid, his eyes glassy. He moaned. In one hand he clutched the bottle of scotch he had shared with Della, empty now. His foot caught on Grove's elbow, and he tripped and landed on his knees. He dropped the bottle then and wrapped his hands around one of Grove's legs. His mouth stretched open to bite into it.

Grove shouted. He forced himself onto his back, breaking Foley's grip.

"Lord, help me!" the warden cried.

Gamewood rushed across the room and kicked Foley in the chest, tumbling him backward into the office. Grove scrambled away on all fours, slipping on the wet floor, dropping back onto his hands and knees each time he tried to stand. Gamewood grabbed him under the arms, helped him up. Foley's moaning, hissing corpse filled the doorway then staggered toward Gamewood. The guard stood with his back to it, off-balance while he stretched to support Grove. Della swung the mop around, planted the head against Foley's abdomen, and shoved with her full weight. The doctor jolted into his office again, tripped over a chair, and landed on his back on the floor.

"Stop him," Grove screamed.

Della withdrew the mop. The sight of Foley dead crushed her. On his desk a bottle of pills lay turned over, its contents scattered. Beside it was a hypodermic needle, a bubble of fluid still in the syringe. *Bastard*, Della thought, and then she slammed the door closed.

Seconds later, the dead doctor banged against the other side.

"What happened?" said Grove.

"He died in there," Gamewood said.

"Obviously, you idiot. But how? Heart attack?"

"The dead nurse cut him," Gamewood said. "Did he bleed to death?"

"The wound wasn't that bad," Della said.

"Did one of those things bite him?"

Della did not want to tell them what she had seen or what Foley said to her before he closed his office door for the last time. The urge to sob, to break down crying almost overwhelmed her, but she held it in check through her anger. Although a small part of her understood it, Foley's cowardice infuriated her. She had believed he was a better man, a stronger one, but he was like almost every other man she had ever known and dared to admire: weak and selfish. Della checked the clock. In a few more hours it would be time to meet the others at the loading dock.

"Did one of those things bite him?" Grove asked again, but no one answered. "I suppose it doesn't matter. Dead is dead. What do we do with him?"

Della said, "Unless you plan to grab a knife and start cutting, *we* do nothing. Gamewood and I, however, will dispose of Doctor Foley's corpse properly."

Grove scowled at Della. He noticed his suit was streaked with blood from his scramble across the floor. He swept a red clump from his sleeve.

"As you wish, Ms. Townsend. The infirmary is now yours to run. Let's you and I talk again soon, in my office, where we won't be interrupted."

Grove walked out. Della stared at Foley's door.

The thing on the other side pounded against it with a rhythm like a slow, steady heartbeat, and Della almost laughed at the irony.

CORNELL:
SIXTEEN

One of the first supplicants at that night's service was a low-level drug trafficker I'd met a few times many years ago and hadn't seen or heard of since. He winked at me and said how it was good to go out with a familiar face nearby. He was small and he burned fast in the bonfire. I hoped they'd all go quick and easy like that so I could be done, keep my rendezvous with Klug and the others, and get gone for good from living in the shadow of Warden Lane Grove.

The second wave included Baldwin, crossing the platform as straight and tall as he could, looking like one of the few who hadn't needed the warden's gentle coercion. I suppose I'd helped out somewhat in that department. He stared me down the whole time, and when the executioner fitted his hood, he flashed me a final smile that said he'd found a way to cheat me out of killing him. Guess it meant something to him, then, how he died. I wasn't sorry to see him go. He deserved to die uglier than he did.

Eighteen more cons took the long dive that night.

One prayed up until the moment the noose choked his throat closed.

Another pranced around and flipped us the bird while he shouted about how he'd see us all in Hell. That one landed in the pen.

There were nine wormfeeders crowded in there, bouncing off each other like catalyzed molecules, but the cage was too strong for them break free. Most of them had worked their hoods loose by now, and they never took their eyes off the crowd, never stopped staring at the living with that stark need that somehow crept up from their empty guts to shape their contorted expressions. I knew, then, the real reason for Mason's brand of target practice. We watched the dead die. They watched us live. A man could only be looked at that way for so long before he needed to react. I was glad I'd be leaving soon.

My first chance to slip away came when the service ended and Grove left the platform. Before I made it, one of the guards caught me dead on, and said, "Warden wants to see you."

Walking through the quiet corridors, I wondered what new torture Grove had devised for me, and I swear I heard the sniff and sensed the heat of the jackal's breath at the side of my face. I felt him nearby almost every hour of the day now, a dark, patient presence waiting for the weight of the mistakes I'd made to finally trap me for him. I promised myself—whatever came, whatever Grove threw at me—I wouldn't go down without a fight. One way or another, I would put my days of self-despair and licking my wounds behind me. Guess I should've known better than to go making promises to myself where the Warden Grove was involved. Down in his office he waited for me with half a dozen hacks, and I knew it had all gone to shit when I saw Old Corntooth cowering in a corner with a bitter, self-satisfied gleam in his wrinkled, dewy eyes.

"Think they're worried about you yet?" he asked. "Mr. Klug and the others don't like to be kept waiting, I'd imagine."

"Don't know what you mean," I said.

"Don't lie to me, Mr. Cornell. You can't protect them. Your old acquaintance already told us about the breakout, but he doesn't know the specifics. Now, I've seen a side of you that others have not, and so I'm willing to give you the benefit of the doubt and believe you were with left no choice but to go along with Mr. Klug's desperate scheme. Now, please, justify my faith in you, and tell me where to find these unrepentant sinners?"

Smart thing to do would have been to give them up to work myself in tight with Grove and bide my time till we left on his mission. I owed Klug nothing. He had only drafted me for his plan and would never have bothered with me if I didn't have something he wanted. It wasn't misguided loyalty that led me the other way. I'd simply had my fill of letting other people call the shots for me. Even if I went down right then, Klug's group would still have a chance to escape without me, and there had to be places other than Lohatchie that might be safe. Mostly, though, I hated to see some tired, broken-down pussy like Old Corntooth get a leg up on the few people I knew who weren't afraid to keep pushing for something other than the shit deal life handed them. And, of course, I had a singular dislike of the warden.

"Nobody's breaking out," I said. "What's the point? Where would they run?"

"Once down this road should've been enough for you, but I see we haven't made the progress I'd hoped." Grove waved on the guards. "I've never been one to shy away from a difficult case, though. All dogs can be trained."

No way was I going to let them kick the shit out of me again. I kissed a little farewell off to Evelyn, an apology for letting it end like this, so pitiful and mundane. I wondered if she might be waiting for me on the other side, not that I believed in all the God and afterlife hoodoo that Grove liked to shill—but damned if that wouldn't make everything all right and send all the pain away if I got to see her again.

Three of the hacks slid batons from their belts.

One tried to draw me out with a loose snap on his holster, an exposed gun inviting me to grab it and give them a reason to start pounding me. Then I wondered why they needed a pretense when the only law left was Grove's and he had brought them all here to beat on me. I glanced at the hack's badge: Georges. The only guard in on the breakout I hadn't yet met. The King Snake's specialty was making things happen; he was as much a clockmaker as a killer. There was no signal in Georges's steady gray eyes, but there couldn't be. He needed me to make the first move. Wouldn't pay for him to blow his cover if I wasn't smart enough to follow his lead and ballsy enough to risk the only option left for me.

Either way the gun offered me a way out.

I prayed it was the one I wanted.

When Georges raised his stick, I seized his automatic, dropped to the floor, rolled, and fired four shots. Three hit home and three guards went down. Before I had time to finish wondering if I'd made the right choice, Georges clubbed the fourth guard to his knees. The fifth froze in his tracks, confronted by the barrel of the gun in my hand. Georges produced a pistol from his back-up holster and aimed it at the warden. The amount of blood staining Grove's carpet told us at least two of the men I'd shot were dead. We all realized it together. Every man in the room glanced at the clock above the door. The countdown began.

Grove stood solid and stone-faced behind his desk. "What exactly do you think you're doing, men?"

"Fuck you, preacher," Georges said. "Consider this a changing of the guard."

"You won't accomplish anything this way except a lot of bloodshed," said Grove. "I'm not afraid to die. How about you? Or you, Mr. Cornell? You going along with this nonsense? Hell, boy, you're one of the few in this place who's actually got a future ahead of him."

I squinted, amazed. "What future? Prancing around like your trained dog?"

"Doing the Lord's work in these trying times. Working toward your redemption."

"Shit!" Georges shouted. "We don't have time for this! And I got no patience for snitches."

He whirled and fired a round into Old Corntooth's head. The impact from the slug knocked him hard against the wall. He slid to the floor, smearing a track of blood behind him. His eyes and his gap-toothed mouth hung wide open.

"I'm sorry, Fredericks. You threw in with the wrong side," Georges said to the last guard. Then he shot him in the chest.

"Cool it, man," I said. "Don't screw things up now."

"You don't tell me what to do," Georges said.

He lunged across Grove's desk and whacked the warden behind the ear with the grip of his pistol. The blow staggered Grove. Georges grabbed him and dragged him out of the office. I followed, slamming the door behind us.

"Leave Grove," I said. "He'll slow us down."

Georges' eyes narrowed, and he glared at me. "Who the fuck asked you, pretty boy? You do what I say."

I was grateful to be out, but Georges was feeling the strain, and I had no idea how high his breaking point was. So I shut up and let him take the lead. We followed the safest route from Grove's office off the administration wing, keeping out of sight along shortcuts and back corridors that Georges knew. Closer we got to the delivery docks the more deserted the way became. The entrance was right where Klug had showed us on his map and the whole area seemed utterly abandoned. In the garage and loading area were only Mason and Combest, piling packages of food onto the back of the truck.

When Mason saw Grove, he dropped the box in his hands. It split open against the floor. A can of peaches rolled out.

"What the fuck is he doing here?" Mason said.

"Klug here, yet?" said Georges.

"No," Mason told him. "Now, tell me why Grove is."

Georges kicked Grove down the stairs. The warden stumbled then fell to the concrete floor where he lay on his back, groaning.

"Get me some rope, Combest," Georges said.

Combest dug a line out of the supplies in the truck and handed it over. Georges tied Grove's hands behind his back, knotted his feet together, and dumped him in a corner.

"Dammit," Mason said. "I'm not playing with you. Why is Grove here?"

"I don't answer to you," Georges said. "Wait for Klug. Let him do the explaining."

Mason didn't like it, but he didn't press things with Georges. I figured he knew the man well enough to know how close he might be to snapping. The way he paced the room while I helped Combest and Mason pack the truck, I figured it couldn't take much more to push him over the edge.

Mason had come through with a stash of rifles, shotguns, and pistols. I tossed Georges empty weapon on the pile. With visible reluctance, Mason handed me a fresh automatic, and—damn the irony—it was a Beretta M9.

"Like you said, gonna have to trust you sometime," Mason told me, flashing a weather eye on Georges.

Fuck, I thought, *how long can these shitkickers keep it together?*

I made sure the Beretta was loaded, thumbed off the safety, and tucked it into my waistband.

Scopes and Della arrived next with two satchels of medical supplies, which Della locked in a chest built into the back of the van. She also brought a black briefcase, which she stowed in the truck. That made all of us, except for Klug and Paulson, and so we sat in the dimly lit garage and waited, most of us maybe wondering what kind of world we'd find outside the walls.

Not me, though.

I knew better.

The world I knew had been stillborn, except for the few shining lights I'd found in it, and I'd allowed the brightest of those to be snuffed out. I didn't expect to find much different out there from when I'd first left it other than a harder road to survival. I didn't care. All I wanted was my freedom. I'd come to prison wanting punishment for letting Evelyn down. Instead I got the same bullshit that kept me from living my life in the first place. Debasing my spirit was never going to help me reconcile my broken promises. Evelyn would've wanted me to live the best life I could on my terms, and that was exactly what I planned to do, what we all planned to do, for as long as we could among the dead. Too bad that jackal sniffing his hot nose through my hair didn't give a puddle of piss about our plans.

SEVENTEEN

We knew right away something was wrong when Paulson shuffled onto the loading platform stiff-legged and gray.

"Shit, he's dead," Mason said. He braced a rifle against his shoulder and squinted into the sight. "No one will hear if I fire. No one's even in this end of the building."

No one objected. Bullets gouged through Paulson's eyes and ripped open most of his skull. He crumpled then rolled over and dragged himself forward, falling from the loading platform to the floor with a wet splat.

"How do we get out of here? Paulson was supposed to have the keys," Combest said.

"Doesn't matter. Wait for Klug," Georges said.

"Maybe Paulson got the stuff before he croaked," Mason said. "Son of a bitch looks like he died on his feet. Must have been sick or something."

"Yeah, he was," I said, remembering how he'd been sweaty and trembling the day he brought me out of solitary.

Mason got a shotgun from the truck and edged toward Paulson. He pressed the barrel against the dead man's left hip and fired, nearly severing the joint. The shot knocked Paulson flat, and Mason shifted the gun over the dead guard's right shoulder and took off an arm. He reloaded and blasted the other, then sighted on Paulson's neck, and ripped the corpse's head most of the way loose. It didn't stop Paulson but he couldn't move very well after that, and Mason found little trouble beating off the advances of the dead man's wiggling limbs while he searched his uniform.

"Got it," he said.

An overloaded key ring dangled from his fingers. In the same hand, he clutched a blood-spattered notebook. He wiped it clean on his pants and opened it. The punch codes were written inside.

"We got everything we need," said Della. "Let's go."

"No!" Georges said. "We do nothing without Klug."

"Klug could be dead or worse," said Della. "The longer we wait—"

Georges slapped her. The smack resounded through the garage. Della staggered.

Mason and I moved at the same time, but I was closer and that's why Georges wound up on the floor with my foot on his throat rather than with a bullet in his head. Mason sure as hell meant to kill him. Someone needed to take control of this free-for-all before things got out of hand.

"Mason," I said, "point your gun somewhere else, give Combest the keys then get the truck ready."

"Fuck you, con. Step aside," said Mason.

Falling back on the tone of voice I'd used to corral terrified bank customers, I looked Mason in the eye, and said, "Mason, you dumb, ugly motherfucker, this is where things either break our way and we make a daring escape into the night or they go to shit and we all die really fucking painful deaths. Give Combest the keys and get the goddamn truck ready. Now!"

He hated me and he didn't want to do it. The give and take passed through his eyes while he weighed his response. I could almost read his thoughts in his face. He was thinking he could kill me and Georges easy with two or three quick shots, but then he'd have to answer to Klug and maybe the others. He lowered his weapon and did what I'd told him. For a moment, I felt like maybe we had a chance of getting out of there.

Combest took five tries to find the right key and open the lock on the loading dock. The electric doors crawled upward. Night poured in, and a narrow driveway stretched out toward it, turning into the darkness in the direction of the prison gate. I expected that fresh air to smell like freedom. Instead I choked on its stench. We couldn't see the wormfeeders, but we could smell them.

"What the hell?" Scopes said.

Three figures drifted toward the open doors. Four more followed. Scopes grabbed a flashlight and caught one full on in the beam—the fat Aryan punk whose neck I'd gouged. His partner trailed behind him. More figures staggered into the faint light. Among them were the victims of some of the cons who'd committed suicide, inmates who'd died less publicly than those in Grove's showcase sacrifices, and some guards who'd maybe refused to go along with the warden's plan. Guess he'd dumped them all here for cheap security in case anyone tried to do what we had in mind. About fifty of them blocked our path. Grove must have started stockpiling them early.

"What do we do, now?" Combest said.

"First of all, close that goddamn door." Klug's voice boomed down from the loading platform. "And Cornell, get your foot off of Georges."

The King Snake approached like his namesake: sly, easy, and lethal. He crouched over Warden Grove and lifted his face from the ground.

"Gotcha, motherfucker. *I win*," he said. Then he punched Grove in the nose and bounced his head off the floor.

Georges got back on his feet. "Son of a bitch, it worked."

"Damn right," the King Snake said. "Now get those guns off the truck and get ready. Y'all ain't going anywhere."

"What the fuck are you talking about?" Mason said.

"We have Grove. That means this whole fucking pit is ours," Klug said. "We put the warden out for show on his own damn gallows, hang his ass out where anyone who wants to can beat his twitching carcass with a stick day and night until it rots away to scraps, and every man in this place will be in our pocket. I have men waiting for my signal. Now I have guns to give them. We're going to turn this place into a fortress."

"And the King Snake will take his throne," I said.

Klug smiled, missing my sarcasm or ignoring it.

"What about escaping?" Della asked.

"To some cabin in the woods? When we can stay here, forage in town, and build an empire? I never wanted to leave, sweetcheeks. Just wanted Grove looking the other way long enough for us to get close to him. Knew he was interested in Cornell so I played that card for what it was worth, and it paid off better than I expected. Escaping was a last ditch backup plan. If shit went south, we could always run." Klug glanced at me and winked. "Sorry I couldn't let you in on it, brother, but I needed you believing we were leaving for real when Grove moved on you. Now, you all can do what I say and come along for the ride or you can die right here and go sit outside with the rotbags."

"This is bullshit," Mason said.

"Think so?" Klug asked.

He took Georges's gun and fired before anyone could stop him. Combest screamed once then fell, clutching at his chest. Klug moved across the room, kicked Combest's body outside then hit the door switch. The panels crawled downward. Combest was still alive, moaning, too shocked to move, as the door shut him out of sight.

"I said close the fucking door," Klug said. He removed the keys from the control box and put them in his pocket.

It wouldn't have hurt the King Snake to let us go, but he wasn't one to give anything away for free. Maybe if he'd known that Mason's family had been among the bus refugees turned out by Grove at the prison gates, he'd have tapped someone else to secure his arsenal, but even I didn't know that then. If Klug had he might've understood Mason felt the same way I did: he only wanted his freedom and he didn't care what anyone else thought he ought to be doing or what anyone else wanted. Damn hard to bully someone who's got nothing to lose and nothing really to gain. No past, no future. A man in that position tends to hit back where it hurts most.

"Well fuck you, too!" Mason yelled.

He raised his shotgun and blew away most of Lane Grove's face in spray of shot and red gore that drenched the concrete.

Klug gaped. "Motherfucker!"

Not even the King Snake could think of everything.

Scopes charged toward the stash of weapons on the truck, but Mason opened up the other barrel and blasted his legs, crippling him.

Georges pulled a snub-nose from his ankle and fired wild, shattering one of the truck windshields. Shots ricocheted off the masonry and everyone ducked. I grabbed Della's arm and pulled her around the far side of the truck we'd loaded. Mason vanished behind one of the other vehicles, firing fast to force Klug and Georges behind a stack of crates in the opposite corner. They left Scopes writhing in pain on the floor. When the echoes of gunfire ceased I heard two things: the lazy thumps of wormfeeders beating against the garage door and the angry voices of living men coming from the inside corridor.

Up to then that jackal breathing down my neck had only been playing with his food. Now his hunger had finally outweighed his boredom, and his jaws were closing.

The inside doors of the loading area exploded with a crash and a whoosh of hot smoke. Six guards burst through in a gray haze. Klug and Georges opened fire before the hacks got their bearings, forcing them back. Two of them dropped on the platform. Georges spread some cover fire while Klug wriggled out and grabbed an automatic rifle off one of the dead, and then the King Snake unleashed his fury. The guards fired back. Bullets whined through the air. Sparks flew as lead pocked the metal doorframe. Bits of concrete spun loose from the walls. Klug's mouth hung wide in a silent scream. He paid no attention to a shot that grazed his shoulder and left a trail of blood soaked into his singed shirtsleeve. Below the crossfire Paulson's head wobbled like a rolling bird's egg. His eyes strained for sight of food. His limbs flopped and squirmed around him like suffocating fish.

Klug and Georges would run out of ammo soon at the rate they were firing, and when their guns died, the guards would advance. Seemed wasteful and stupid until I understood they were watching the clock, holding off the hacks till the dead men on the platform got up and started running interference. Might have done the same myself. That thought got me moving, because I knew the next step would be to get to the weapons, and unless Klug's disposition had gotten a whole lot cheerier as a result of being shot and losing his sacrificial prize pig, that meant going through us. Mason and I made eye contact, drawing the same conclusion: our only way out was the yard.

We had the truck. Klug had the keys to the door.

"Can you shoot?" I asked Della.

She nodded. I shoved my gun into her hands and told her to cover me.

"Okay," she said.

She handled the gun with confidence, getting a shot off every few seconds to keep Georges from turning his attention our way. I slipped into the exposed opening at the back of the truck and found the three spare fuel cans that had been stocked up. I lined them up within reach of the door, grabbed one, dropped to the floor, ducked, and crab-walked toward the yard exit. The pungent fumes burned my nose when I opened the cap. I tried not to splash fuel on myself as I emptied the can to make a puddle halfway along the length of the door. The wormfeeders stood just inches away on the far side. Their sad moans drifted through, and the metal rattled under their fists.

Running back to Della, I saw Warden Grove's corpse stand up. The remains of his head poked upward like a broken flower-pot, and he shuffled his way toward the nearest food source: Scopes. Grove pounced on the wounded con like a rat, ripping his flesh with his splintered teeth. Scopes fought but he had lost a lot of blood and was weak. Probably slipping into shock, too, and likely run through with horror at watching himself being eaten. He only stopped screaming when Grove chewed his throat open and champed down on his larynx.

The gunshots died down. Georges had emptied his snub-nose and produced yet another weapon, and I wondered where the hell he hid them all. A truck engine rumbled to life. Mason sat behind the wheel of the vehicle he'd been using for cover. I had time to wave to him once for luck before he revved the motor, popped the clutch, and blasted in reverse across the loading area. The truck body smashed through the crates that had shielded Klug and Georges. Chunks of wood whirled in every direction. Klug twisted around, his face a contorted mask of surprise as the back bumper caught him below the waist, lifted him and pinned him to the cinder-block wall. His rifle sailed loose and disappeared below the wheels. I thought the impact might cut him in half, but then the truck came to an abrupt halt.

The crash left Georges sprawled sideways in a mess of broken crates. He tried to aim his gun when Mason climbed out of the cab, but his hand drooped from his broken wrist like a useless toy. Mason shot him, hitting him in the neck. Georges pressed his shattered hand against the wound and tried to hold back the gout of blood streaming out.

I grabbed a shotgun from the stash and trailed Della to the corner. We got there in time to watch the King Snake realize that he was trapped unarmed with a corpse that would soon be hungry for his flesh and that we were going to leave without him. He didn't like either circumstance.

Mason shoved his hand into Klug's sweat-dampened shirt pocket, fishing for the keys. When he found them, he took them straight to the control box. We needed to run. Soon it would dawn on the supercops in the corridor that they weren't being shot at anymore, and then they'd recover their bravery.

"You can't leave me here, Cornell," said Klug. "I know this shit wasn't supposed to go down this way, but we've got to put that behind us. C'mon, man. I never did you no wrong. Used you a little, yeah, but you were going to be there with me at the top. Ain't no part of Lohatchie left but you and me. We got to stick together. How else we gonna survive this crazy shit? Just fucking help me, man, all right?"

Felt like I should've had something smart to say then, but nothing came to mind. I stared at Klug like he was a bug pinned to piece of corkboard. His face screwed into a twisted wreck of anger and pain, and then all at once let it go as he started laughing. Only took me a moment to catch onto the joke.

I ducked sideways with maybe a half second left to avoid the gore-drenched hug of Warden Grove approaching me from behind. Klug stopped laughing when Grove's momentum carried him into the wreckage. The dead preacher tripped, plunged forward, and started scrabbling his way toward the King Snake. After all, what's the difference between Klug and me to a wormfeeder? Fresh meat is fresh meat.

With the corner of my eye I spotted the two dead hacks dragging their pale bodies upright on the platform.

Scopes would be next.

Time to move.

Della sent a couple of potshots at the guards to keep them hiding then ran to the truck. Mason was ready at the control box.

My first two matches extinguished in the gas puddle, but the third ignited a low wall of blinding hot flame that licked at the door. Mason hit the switch and we hauled back to the getaway truck as the door inched up. The fire spread down a ten-foot length between us and the yard, and as the opening widened, the first wormfeeders pushed inside. They burned like jack o' lanterns, and the aroma of cooking flesh polluted the air. Others fell into the conflagration and drove the flames higher. The smart ones trailed around to the clear end. Soon nearly all the corpses had shambled to one side and the yard emptied out in front of us.

The first wormfeeder to reach the truck knocked on the passenger side window and Mason gave him the finger. Della hunkered down behind the seat and I sat behind the wheel with the engine running. Only three wormfeeders stood in our way when I gunned the motor. Heat rippled through the truck as we breached the waist-high fire. The dead things crunched under the tires, bouncing us like speed bumps, as we emerged into the yard. Then Mason was pulling my arm and screaming, tugging on the wheel so we swerved right and smacked more wormfeeders off our fenders.

Combest's body appeared in the glow of the headlights.

The punch codes.

I slammed the brakes hard and brought the passenger side as close to Combest as I could. The truck skidded. For a fleeting second two right tires left the ground, and I felt certain we'd tip and crash, but then gravity sucked the vehicle back down and it jolted to a shuddering stop. Mason popped the door and dropped to the ground. He fired on the closest wormfeeders, launching chunks of flesh into the darkness, then rifled Combest's shirt. The notebook was gone. He heaved the body over and patted the dark grass, feeling for the paper and cardboard. The wormfeeders closed in. I slid into the passenger seat and blasted them with the scattergun. Stale blood spit from their wounds, but they kept coming. In moments they'd overrun us.

"Forget it," I shouted. "We'll crash the gate."

"No!" Mason called back. "Got it!"

Combest grabbed him before he could stand. His body shivered as movement returned to it, and he came at Mason with his mouth open, teeth bared. Mason tripped trying to scramble away. He strained to aim his gun at Combest, but they were pressed too close together. The other wormfeeders closed on them. In the half second I took to think of leaping out of the truck and helping Mason instead of hitting the gas and running, Della raised her gun and fired into Combest, forcing him away from Mason.

The next moment, Mason was back in the cab, shoving me toward the driver's seat and tugging the door closed behind him. I punched the gas and we rocketed into the yard, plowing through wormfeeders. The truck jounced and skidded. Twice, bodies caught up on the wheels almost sent us out of control, but after that the ride smoothed out as we raced down the hard pavement of the driveway. The first fence loomed ahead, a darkened guard post beyond it, and I skidded us to a halt two inches from the heavy chain link.

Mason leapt out, clutching the wet notebook and punched in the codes. The wormfeeders came faster than I thought they could. A dozen wobbled toward us.

"Shit, there are more of them?" said Della.

Mason sidestepped the rolling gate to enter the pen, and I edged the truck in after him. I jumped out with a rifle once we were in the tight space of the checkpoint. The fence slid closed after us. We sat sandwiched between the yard and the outside world. We looked at our exit, sealed by a single chain-link gate topped with razor wire, the only thing between us and the whole goddamn, dead-infested world. There, beyond the gate, seventy, eighty, a hundred wormfeeders glommed against the aluminum mesh like they'd been expecting us all along.

Mason roared and fired round after round into them till he emptied his magazine. I thought he might reload and keep firing, but instead he slung the rifle over his shoulder and rubbed his eyes.

"Fuck. How the hell do we get past them?"

Della climbed out of the cab. "What now?"

"Now," I said. "We blow up the truck."

I don't know why I said it. It was the first thing I thought of and it struck me as the kind of rare inspiration that should be trusted even if you can't quite picture how it's all going to work out. I didn't know what chance we'd have on foot outside the prison walls, but I heard Evelyn's voice in my mind telling me not to give up, happy again because I'd stopped lying down to take whatever came my way. Or as Lane Grove might have put it, the Lord helps those who help themselves.

"That's the best you can come up with?" Della said.

"Yeah," I told her. "Go back, we die. Stay here, we die. Only choice we've got is keep going forward. We've come too far to do anything else. Unless we take out a whole bunch of the dead in our path all at once, going forward is going to be a tad difficult."

She turned to Mason, who shrugged.

"I got nothing better to suggest," he said.

"Sonofabitch," she said. "Couple of geniuses I wound up with. Let's make it work."

"We take what we can carry," I said. "Then light the gas tank, open the gate, and hide in the station booth. Let in as many wormfeeders as will fit and wait for the fuel to blow them to cinders. Then we run out through the visitor's door and haul ass across the meadow behind them. They've been gathering around the prison for so long, maybe they won't be so dense once we get some distance."

The guard station included a small airlock type of arrangement that protruded beyond the gate. It was used to admit people on foot without passing them through the pen. It wouldn't protect us for long, but I hoped it wouldn't have to. The chain link on either side of us buckled under the weight of the dead. They saw us. They wanted us. On the yard side, I saw Scopes and Grove in with the crowd, and I saw Klug in the distance limping along with half his torso shorn open. Seeing Grove's ruined body lurch against the fence, I wondered if the warden had met his god now, even though there was no bonfire for him, only the pen.

"Town's thirty miles north of here," said Mason. "Gonna be a hard run across countryside crawling with wormfeeders. My house is less than half that distance east. We make it there, we can get a car."

"All right," I said. "Mason's serving breakfast. Let's start packing."

We took guns and extra ammo from the truck. Della insisted on bringing the medical supplies. I figured any wound you couldn't walk off was as good as being dead, but I didn't argue. We stowed enough food to hold us for at least three days, and Della retrieved the black briefcase she'd brought.

"What's in there?" I asked.

"Information," she said. "Doctor Foley's laptop. It's a piece of military equipment with a link to a satellite network."

"How the hell did Foley come by that?"

"Worked for the CDC," she said.

"Hunh. Maybe it'll be useful," I said. "Hope you remembered to grab the charger."

Della's face blanked for a moment before it twisted with anger. "Dammit," she said. "Sonofabitch."

"Don't sweat it. We'll figure something out. If not, it looks heavy—you can use it as a club."

Fuming, Della put the briefcase with the rest of our things in the airlock, and then we prepared the truck.

Fetid hands clawed the chain link on both sides of us. The cries and groans of the dead filled the air. Mason and Della put our gear in the guardhouse while I tied together strips of padding from the truck and soaked them in gas to make a fuse. I threaded it into the truck's gas nozzle and shoved it down as deep as I could with my rifle barrel. Della took the third can of gas, jumped up on the hood of the truck, and splashed fuel over the mob of wormfeeders until they were soaked and dripping, shining in the moonlight. Mason entered the code for the gate and punched the button. It creaked sideways, squealing under the weight of the dead.

I lit the fuse. We ran into the booth.

Wormfeeders stumbled in, pushing and shoving, tripping over one another in the confined space. The gates spread and more followed, clotting against the front of the truck and blotting out the headlights. The pen became a writhing tangle of shadows creeping toward the guard booth, where we crouched below the window level. I crossed my fingers hoping the wire-reinforced glass would hold up to the explosion.

Damn good thing it at least proved bullet resistant.

Three shots must have struck it before we realized we were under fire.

The spotlight in the nearby guard tower flickered to life and we saw hacks up there pointing down at us.

The light drew the attention of the wormfeeders away from the booth, but there were so many of them, there was no way to return fire without exposing ourselves. We were stuck waiting, and it was taking a hell of lot longer than I had expected for the gas tank to blow. We heard the dead right on top of us, lowing like sick cows and batting weak fists against the windows. They knew we were there and it was stoking their hunger. Every few seconds another shot from the guard tower ripped through one of the dead and sprayed blood onto the window glass, turning the glow from the spotlight beam ruby-red in our dark hiding space. The gunshots came faster. The windows couldn't hold much longer. Splinters of glass cracked loose and sprayed around us. We grabbed our weapons and prepared to fight the living and the dead.

Night erupted into blinding day.

A wave of heat cascaded over us.

The weakened glass shattered, and heavy, webbed chunks rained down. Burning metal and flesh flew into the room and crashed against the far wall.

The explosion had been less powerful than I expected. The truck went up like a charcoal barbecue doused with too much lighter fluid rather than a bomb, but it achieved the desired effect. All the wormfeeders in the pen lit up from head to toe, packed so close together that the flames danced among them, reaching out to those still beyond the gate, racing through the dark to turn the mass of them into horrible scarecrow torches. The confines of the pen had driven much of the explosive force upward where it hit the guard tower. The spotlight went dark when a piece of debris shattered it. Patches of flame burned in the darkness above us.

We ran.

Four wormfeeders lingered outside the visitor's door. Mason shoved his shotgun into one's mouth and fired. The corpse's decomposed skull muffled the blast as it burst. Della shot another one in the leg and toppled it. I pounded at the other two with the stock of my rifle, beating them aside and forcing them to the ground. More wormfeeders came toward us, but we batted them away or shot their feet out from under them. The farther we moved from the prison, the fewer we met. Most of them had their attention elsewhere. Trundling toward the gate were two ragged lines of walking dead coming around the prison walls, drawn by the light and noise or beckoned by those who'd been there first. Their horrible voices filled the night.

We followed a path through the woods, one Mason knew well enough to navigate in the dark, and came out on the road two miles away from the prison. It was deserted. At a steady pace, we'd reach Mason's house by morning. There we could figure out what came next. One thing Klug got right was my hideaway deep in the Everglades north of Lohatchie. If all the world proved a cesspool of decaying flesh and cannibal corpses, then we could head there, leave it all behind us, and maybe make a new life. Maybe not. I wasn't one to count on a happy ending, no matter how simple it sounded.

Walking along in the moonlit stillness, I tasted air free of rot and fear for the first time in weeks. I knew again how it felt to be my own man. Somewhere that smiling jackal laughed over the good scare he gave me, knowing all along it was only a matter of time before he decided to deliver what he'd promised. For now, though, it was enough that I could no longer hear Evelyn's voice in the back of my mind. That's how I knew she was pleased.

BIRCH'S REFUGEES

A man in ragged, red clothes walked among the dead.

No, *not* a man. A corpse.

That James Birch thought of him as a man at first glance made him extraordinary. He didn't move like the other walking corpses, who wandered the field below the hospital like shell-shocked survivors, tripping over scattered piles of fallen bodies. Rather, the man in red moved with a purpose and an alertness alien among the living dead. But Birch had no doubt he *was* dead; the signs of decay on his face and arms were modest but unmistakable. And any living man who walked that field would've been quartered and devoured by the dead in minutes—yet they paid no attention to the man in red. To them he was only another rotting body among the dead masses.

His actions astonished Birch more than his appearance. As he worked his way across the field, he knelt beside one damaged corpse after another, lingering long enough only to press his fingers against each one's eyes, like a priest delivering a final blessing. Hundreds of bodies littered that field, decay hardened, capable only of twisting and wriggling in the mud because their legs and arms had been shattered or severed in a battle Birch hadn't witnessed; from the hospital roof, they looked like frantic, broken ants. But once the dead man knelt by them—once he touched them—they turned stone still and didn't rise.

Truly dead.

Birch would've killed or died to know how to do what the man in red did. Almost any living man would've.

The cloudless afternoon darkened for a breath, and Birch shivered. A kind of energy radiated from the strange dead man, rising in ripples of palpable cold that sought something, sought...*life*. It connected with Birch in a jolt at the base of his neck, the touch of a desolate consciousness swollen with hatred and insatiable hunger.

The man in red looked up and met Birch's stare across the haze.

Birch froze.

Behind him, a motor started. Propellers whined as the pilot prepped the helicopter for take-off. The soldiers were loading the cargo space with boxes of supplies foraged from the hospital laboratories. Birch held a box of unused Petri dishes filled with agar jelly. He should've been helping to load the huey but he couldn't move. The strange dead man's intense gaze pinned him in place. Worse, it felt familiar.

While his lifeless eyes remained on Birch, the man in red reached for the next corpse: a woman in a torn workout suit, so mottled with stains it resembled a lizard's skin, bisected at the waist. Yet drawn by the helicopter noise and the activity on the roof, her two halves tried to claw and squirm their way toward the hospital and the sounds of life. Then the man in red touched her eyes, and the woman flopped to the ground, both parts of her dead for good. Her savior awaited Birch's reaction, but Birch only gaped, too stunned to express anything. He doubted his own senses. No one else seemed to notice the man in red, not the soldiers hurrying around the rooftop, not the two snipers posted to watch the hospital grounds. Maybe after weeks of haunting his sleep, Birch's dreams of the dead now leaked into his waking life. Or maybe this was another vision, another glimpse between the cracks of reality that only Birch saw.

A cluster of walking corpses mobbed the hospital entrance now. They beat themselves against the doors, pounded them with weak fists, and even the dead who couldn't move yearned to join them. They hungered for flesh, thirsted for blood. Birch wondered if the dead felt pain when they starved. Even severed arms, legs, and heads still shifted around on the ground, worms in the mud, hands dragging themselves forward on rotting fingers, driven by an incomprehensible need to find life and consume it. And at the center of the field, the man in red put down another shattered corpse. Then another. And another after that. Miraculous. Birch wanted to know what the dead felt in the last seconds before their wasting bodies stopped moving, if they felt anything at all.

The man in red held nothing in his hands. He did no more than brush his gray fingertips across the eyes of those he released. Birch wished that power flowed through him.

Certain he had seen the man's face before, he dredged his memory but couldn't recall from where he knew him. Rot obscured his features, and no one ever looked quite the same in living death as they had in life. The cold energy flowing between them surged, driving a frigid spike through Birch's head. He winced as silent words sprang into his thoughts: *You* will *remember me. You killed me. You wouldn't let me serve the living, so now I bring mercy to the dead. Soon you and everyone else will be part of my ministry.*

The voice echoed in Birch's mind, shallow, distorted yet almost recognizable. Another blast of pain expanded in his head. He flinched and dropped the case in his hands. Plastic and glass cracked when it smacked the ground, and the lid snapped open. Birch glanced down at the box then back to the field.

The man in red was gone.

The cold energy dissipated.

"Sir?" Private Lou Nelson stood at Birch's side, eyeing Birch's shaking hands. "You all right, sir?"

Birch hesitated then shook his head. "Fine. Just... tired. I was up all night." He folded the box shut and lifted it.

"See something down there?" Nelson asked.

"Thought I saw a living man walking around."

"Living? No way, not down there," Nelson said. "Some of the rotters still look pretty good, I guess. Probably that's all you saw."

"Maybe."

Birch wanted to find the man in red and make him tell how he killed the dead. If he insisted on what he'd seen, he knew the men would believe him—that they'd hunt for the strange dead man, fight through throngs of the walking dead, even die if he only told them that's what it would take to end the dead plague. Even as Birch thought that, a shred of hope glimmered in Nelson's eyes, so faint the private probably didn't realize it'd crept into his expression. Birch took it for hope that maybe he really had seen something that could help them down amidst the horror.

Maybe I have and maybe I haven't. I don't know what's real anymore.

"A good-looking rotter," he said. "That had to be it."

He stared across the field, the wind of the chopper blades beating at his back. Layered strands of gold and orange clouds stacked on the horizon.

"Sir, just so you know the chopper's loaded, and we'll go whenever you're ready. But, sir, if you don't mind me saying, we'd all like to make it back to Vanguard before sunset."

"Right, me too," Birch said. "Let's split."

He followed Nelson to the helicopter, crouching low as he boarded and shoved the box into a space in the cabin. As the whirlybird rose, Birch studied the field. He'd seen it from the air several times on runs to scavenge supplies, but it had never seemed so placid. Despite the dead clamoring at the hospital doors and the wrecked bodies twitching in the mud, the wide swath of corpses stilled by the man in red made the field look like an overturned graveyard.

If the strange dead man were someone Birch had killed that hardly narrowed the field. He had done a lot of dirty work in his day. He couldn't remember everyone who'd died because of him, and, if he was being honest, he didn't even know who they all were.

He nudged Nelson, sitting beside him, and pointed out the band of unmoving dead bodies. "What do you make of that?"

Nelson shrugged. "Guess they rotted out."

The chopper angled away, and the field dropped from sight. Birch closed his eyes.

The memory of the strange corpse's words stoked his anger. Hard enough these days to sustain belief in life as something worth preserving at any cost, he didn't need the dead invading his mind. He didn't want the dreams and visions of them that came almost every night, didn't want to be the only man with answers for the living. He no longer held any certainty that the answer to the dead plague could ever be known—until today, when he saw what the man in red could do. If all that proved only a waking dream, he feared it might crush his faltering hope for good. The dead had risen and taken over the world, the living were in decline, lights out, curtains closed.

Maybe that was all there was to it.

DAY 17, 1:15 P.M.

The soldiers flattened the dead with tanks; the treads crushed them to dust and jelly, leaving only a scattering of fingers and toes twitching in the mashed earth. Weeks ago, Birch had suggested using lengths of cable to corral the walking corpses and then crushing them with the four M2A3 Bradley's Major Alan Novak commanded. Now the procedure anchored the daily routine at Vanguard labs, and the men cleaned away the remains with flamethrowers. Although not enclosed, the biolab facility stood far enough from the nearest town that not too many corpses found their way there. The "wrap and smash," as the men had named it, had won Birch the Major's confidence. Now he sat in Novak's commandeered office, watching the operation through a window. He admired its simplicity. A direct solution for a clear-cut problem, the absolute opposite of the dilemma he faced in the lab and the favor he hoped Novak would grant him.

"The *Clostridium tetani* produces a neurotoxin, called tetanospasmin," Birch told Novak. "It ravages living muscle and skeletal fibers, causing the muscular contractions and lockjaw of tetanus. Theoretically, a modified form of the bacteria could produce an attenuated toxin that might explain the controlled movements of the walking dead. They could mimic life through bacteria-driven muscular contractions."

"It's mutant tetanus? That's the cause?" Novak jotted notes on a pad at the center of his well-ordered desk. "Can I report that to General Collier?"

"No. Nothing's certain. The bacteria and toxin are present in the tissue samples I've studied, but the rest is only a hypothesis," Birch said. "Part of one, at least. It doesn't explain why they attack and eat the living, why they move around like they do, why they migrate, and why they're not rotting on their bones. If reanimation was due to bacteria alone, their movements would be random, and they'd be decomposing at a normal rate. This might be *how* the dead are walking, but it isn't the only factor. It isn't *why* they're walking."

"What's the difference?"

"You drop a bomb on a target, that's *how* you destroy it, right?" Birch said. "The reason you drop that bomb, the reason it exists in the first place, those are separate things. The bomber might not even know why he's using it. To him, the bomb is only a tool."

"Are you telling me this is an attack, the bacterium is a bioweapon?"

"No. This wasn't created in a lab."

"Fuck's sake, Birch. Make yourself clear. I've been cutting you serious slack since I got here, because you were Special Forces back in the day and you seem like the only one with his head screwed on right about this clustershtup. But I need results. The brass are getting nervous, and when the brass get nervous, I get nervous, and that upsets my stomach, which means I can't enjoy that oh-so-important, first cup of coffee in the morning, and that puts me in a rotten damn mood all day, every day. That's no good for anyone. So, fix this shit already, you fucking mad scientist egghead, because I want to know that all is right in the world again so I can enjoy my morning coffee."

Birch waited for the major to smile or laugh; he didn't.

An improbable burst of admiration for the man filled Birch. Confronted by a set of insane circumstances, Novak boiled things down to a simple benchmark for success. That kind of thinking made him an effective soldier, but it would only work for so long. Birch had known other soldiers like Novak, and he knew what might happen when they exhausted their coping mechanism.

"Doing my best, sir." Birch considered telling Novak about his visions, the things he saw in his dreams, even about the dead man in red, but Novak wouldn't believe him. It would only give him cause to doubt Birch's sanity and that would complicate everything. "This thing isn't exactly in the textbooks."

"Did it evolve?" Novak said.

"Everything evolves. But, no, not how you mean, centuries of genetic processes happening in days like in some mindless, Hollywood blockbuster, and not because it had a will to evolve or some other nonsense. If it really is the *Clostridium tetani*, it evolved because something in its nature gives this strain an edge in reproducing. If that's where it came from we've been living with it for a long, long time. It's possible. There could have been an animal reservoir before it made the jump to humans, but we'd have seen isolated cases before the dead plague, maybe going back decades, maybe without knowing what they were. It's possible we did and they were misidentified, but I find that unlikely. The symptoms of reanimation are... acute. Anyway, the dead plague wouldn't have come on all at once, spreading in days like it did. It would've taken months, maybe years. Tetanus doesn't spread like the measles."

"Listen, I need something to report," Novak said.

"I know. Thing is, the toxin should be impotent in dead flesh. *Clostridium tetani* is anaerobic. Its spores can survive in dead tissue if it isn't exposed to oxygen. Spores are a far cry from the dynamic bacteria we've found under the microscope, though. You get tetanus when you step on, say, a rusty nail, because it punctures your flesh, delivering the bacteria from within the rust inside your body to an environment that allows it to grow. Something has to be putting this modified bacterium into dead bodies at almost the exact moment of death. Then it replicates and spreads in minutes through the dead tissue in sufficient volume to reanimate the corpse. In my clinical opinion, that's fucking nuts."

"Maybe it's already there when people die. Someone aerosolized it, dispersed it, and people inhaled it."

"No. The fundamental nature of the C. tetani hasn't changed. It's still anaerobic. Prolonged exposure to air would destroy it. I've been taking blood tests from everyone who'll let me, and I haven't found a single living person with it in their system."

"What about your control?"

"Decomposing nicely, no bacteria present, but he hasn't provided any real clues."

"So, what, you hit a dead end already?"

"I've only been at it for two weeks."

"Time is not on our side."

"Talk to Gochek. Talk to Friedman. See what they've learned."

Novak dropped his pen on the desk and leaned back in his chair. " Friedman's got nothing and admits it. Gocheck says it's space dust we picked up from a passing comet."

"He's making that up because you scare him."

"Yes, I do, and that he is. He's an engineer not a biologist, so what can I expect? I have to make due with the available resources. Everything crashed so fast, there was no time to prepare. You're the only one bringing in anything I can wrap my mind around. And here's a sobering thought: you may be the only one in the country with a grasp on this thing. You're the hot ticket. I report to my boss, he reports to his, and he calls the President. You make sense of this thing."

Birch shuddered. "Do I?"

"A mutant bacterium? Yes, I understand that."

"That's not what I said."

"That's what it sounded like. At least, it's a start."

Novak stared Birch down, and the scientist checked himself from disillusioning him. Novak trusted him, and Birch could not say he was wrong. Maybe what he'd learned so far would lead to answers or even a cure.

In the meadow outside, soldiers scrambled near the complex's main entrance. One group provided cover fire for another uncoiling cable between two Jeeps. The shooters destroyed legs and joints with controlled bursts of gunfire, immobilizing the dead, easy prey for the tanks. The line of bodies in the scorched grass reminded Birch of the field outside the hospital, and he thought of the dead man in red, walking from one twitching corpse to another, stilling each one he touched. The key to the dead plague hid in that touch.

"We may have to move soon," Novak said. "The dead are starting to turn up here in bigger groups."

"Let's hold out as long as we can. There's no other lab in this state—hell on this coast—with the equipment we have here. Very little of it is mobile."

"My men are doing their best."

"They're doing incredible. They've kept us safe."

"Another week, though, who knows?" Novak said.

Birch cleared his throat. "One other thing. O'Neal's doing well. She'd like to go back to her room now. That okay with you?"

Novak's expression hardened. "She all healed up?"

"Getting there. She's fine. Really, she is."

Novak shook his head. "Talk to me when her scabs are peeling."

DAY 17, 2:30 P.M.

Birch stood in the parking lot and watched soldiers tighten a cable around thirty or so dead. The corpses moaned and swiped at the living with stiff hands. Then the cable dropped and the group began to push apart, but the tanks rolled in too fast and pressed them to the ground. The Bradleys grumbled with solid, mechanical certainty, leaving behind a slick of decomposed muck and splintered bones. Afterward the soldiers hosed down the tank treads to clean away bits of bodies and clothing. Then they torched the remains left in the grass.

Birch knew Novak's commanders had only sent the tank unit to Vanguard in the first days of the dead plague because they expected equally definitive results on a grand scale. Vanguard specialized in bioscience with military applications, everything from better anthrax vaccines and organic sutures to weaponized allergens and untraceable, fast-degrading bioweapons. Over a decade, the Army had sunk a fortune into the company. As its vice president of research, Birch knew well the give and take of dealing with the military. Their protection would last only as long as he could produce. Until yesterday, he'd feared he'd reached a dead end.

He returned to the main building, to the sub-level where he kept his specimens, carded into the secure corridor, and then waded into a gut-churning stench. The first door on his right led to O'Neal's room, a storage area converted into makeshift quarters. Birch knocked then entered, pushing the door open against towels jammed at its base to block out the smell. O'Neal sat on her bed reading a Douglas Adams paperback. She lowered a cloth soaked with water and perfume from her mouth. Birch sniffed its faint sweetness.

"Please say you've come to bring me upstairs," O'Neal said.

"Novak won't budge until your scabs are peeling."

Birch examined O'Neal's bandages, lifted some to check her wounds.

Wormfeeders had bitten her thirteen times in a dead attack the day Novak's unit arrived. At one point her wounds turned black with infection and O'Neal had languished, feverish, for days, dozens of tooth marks oozing pus and blood, but she'd recovered.

"You're still a little on the wet side, so no go for now. Sorry. How you feeling?"

"Bored out of my skull. At least I barely notice the stink anymore."

"Any cravings for the flesh of the living?"

"I might bite Major Novak's ass if he doesn't let me out of here soon."

"He's playing it safe. Look on the bright side: You've proven the bites themselves aren't fatal or contagious. The risk if you're bitten is dying of blood loss or infection."

O'Neal dog-eared the page she was reading and dropped the book on her bed. Birch picked it up.

"*Life, the Universe, and Everything*? Self-help?"

O'Neal laughed. "I wish. Robbins loaned it to me, but he doesn't have the first two in the series. I read them in high school. Funny stuff. Thought it might cheer me up."

"Don't panic," Birch said.

"Words to live by," O'Neal said. "You need a hand wrangling your specimens?"

Birch shook his head. "No. I only came down for some samples from Dickie, and he's still a well-behaved corpse."

Birch and O'Neal walked to the next storeroom, where Dickie Stein's body was stored. There were five storage rooms in a row along the hall, and the other three held Birch's specimens of the reanimated dead. Sometimes they moaned and banged listlessly on the doors, but now they were silent. Birch looked in on Stein's body. A foul blast of air crept from the room. Birch coughed.

"Still dead," O'Neal said. "Here, use this."

She handed Birch her washcloth. He held it loosely over his mouth and nose, and it filled his nostrils with the sugary aroma of cheap perfume. It cut down the rotten stink, allowing Birch to collect hair and tissue samples from Stein's corpse. Stein, a Vanguard janitor, had dropped dead from a heart attack six days ago while mopping up the labs—but he never got up again. So far Birch had found very little active *Clostridium tetani* in his body. When he had what he needed, Birch slammed the door and returned the cloth to O'Neal.

"I'm so sorry you have to sleep next door to that."

O'Neal shrugged. "Duty calls. Sometimes duty stinks. Besides, it's not a whole lot worse than a boot camp locker room in August. Just has a different *tang* to it."

Birch and O'Neal laughed as they returned to her room. O'Neal flopped onto her bed and whistled. Birch noticed a clean uniform hanging from a hook in the corner, and under it, propped against the wall, stood O'Neal's rifle. One of her fellow soldiers had brought them, a sign they hadn't given up on her. Birch envied her the camaraderie.

"How's life topside?"

"Fine. Except for all the walking dead."

"Worse than mosquitoes."

"We're attracting attention. Fifteen miles from the nearest anything, but we've got more showing up every day. As much as they can know anything, they know we're out here."

"How long can we hold out?"

"Another week, maybe."

O'Neal sat up. "What happens to me if we need to leave in a hurry?"

"You'll be clear in a couple days. If we need to leave before then, I'll come get you myself."

"Thanks. A girl can stand just about anything but to be forgotten."

"No one gets left behind," Birch said. "God only knows where we'll go, though. Hey, you know, I don't even know where you from."

"Virginia."

"Been there a few times."

"You?"

"Long Island."

"We're both pretty far from home."

"You itching to get back there?"

"Yes and no. I've got a big family. I try not to think about what happened to them. Maybe it's better if I never go back. I'm not sure home exists anymore."

"Sorry. Stupid question."

"Forget it. I'm sure you've got the same worries."

"Not really. I haven't had a family for a long time." Birch gathered his samples from where he had set them on the floor and backed out into the corridor. "Rest up. I'll see you later."

Ignoring the awkward sympathy in O'Neal's expression, Birch closed the door behind him.

DAY 25, 9:32 A.M.

Wrapped inside a heavy-duty trash bag, the thing on the worktable thrashed sideways and fell to the floor. The four soldiers who'd set it there seconds ago rushed to retrieve it and replaced it where it belonged. The thing inside twisted and fought, but they held it down tight on the steel table. One of its hands ripped through the bag and clawed at a soldier's wrist with cracked fingernails too weak to penetrate the man's thick work gloves. All of the soldiers wore them, as they wore bandanas across their faces to dampen the stench.

"Hold it in place," Birch said. "I've got to strap it down."

He wore the same type of heavy gloves as the soldiers, the material so thick that his scalpel looked like a toy between his bulky fingers. He sliced away part of the plastic bag, exposing the thing's head and neck. The dead man stared at him with sunken eyes and ground its yellowed teeth. Birch ignored him.

He grabbed one of the nylon straps he'd rigged to the table, pulled it snug across the thing's forehead, and tightened it in place. He drew a second strap across its jaw. Then he cut away more of the plastic bag and strapped the dead thing's shoulders down. With the soldiers' help, he worked his way along the rest of the writhing corpse, pinning it to the worktable, using cuffs for the thing's hands. He stopped at the waist, but only because nothing remained below that. The dead man's legs had been crushed to pulp and amputated during the morning wrap and smash, his upper body preserved from destruction only because Birch had requisitioned a fresh work sample, as he'd done every day for the past five days, since he discovered the first anomaly.

"All right, he's secure," Birch said.

The soldiers backed away to the room's four corners, following Major Novak's orders never to leave Birch unguarded with an active specimen. Lang and McCormick, Birch's assistants, prepared the body for dissection. Lang scissored away the remnants of its clothing and cleaned it of sticks, dirt, and other debris. McCormick set up a video camera on a tripod by the worktable. The dead man's sallow eyes tracked everyone who passed it. Behind its crooked teeth and disintegrating lips, its black tongue rustled and squirmed. The thing moaned, a low, gravelly noise, unbroken even to take a breath, carrying on, rising, falling, producing garbled sounds that sometimes mimicked speech. Birch wadded up a rag and shoved it into the thing's mouth, muting it. He traded his thick work gloves for sterile latex and then approached the specimen.

Birch glanced at the camera. "Tissue samples and general observation of one of the reanimated dead, day 25 of the dead plague. Specimen is male, adult, age...," Birch eyed the corpse for a clue, but found nothing, "...indeterminate. Specimen gathered at Vanguard location during routine security procedure. Time of death and duration of reanimation unknown."

The dead thing showed no reaction when Birch pushed the scalpel into its flesh and cut downward along its chest all the way to its waist. The partly-decomposed skin split like leather. Birch kept up a steady verbal description of his work, recording it for future reference, as he'd recorded dozens of similar dissections. The familiar red light of the camera blinked at him like a metronome. *As if anyone will ever want to watch this.* Still, if he missed an answer right under his nose, he wanted to make sure he had a second chance to find it.

He cracked the body open and began to remove its organs, placing each gray, shriveled piece in containers that Lang readied and then removed. He stacked them on the counter for study later. The heart, lungs, and most of the intestines were gone when Birch noticed the pronounced bulge, like a massive cyst, in the thing's liver. It rotated beneath the surface. Birch set down his scalpel, wiped his face with a paper towel, then rubbed his eyes. He hoped that when he looked again, the thing would be gone.

It wasn't.

About the size of a golf ball, the bulge shifted, rippling the dead flesh that encased it. Birch gestured for McCormick to focus the camera's lens on the liver then he retrieved his scalpel and sliced open the bump. The blade nicked dead meat, and the thing's motion ceased. Birch hesitated. He dreaded what was coming next. The liver parted along the circumference of the cyst; it opened like an eyelid and revealed a dead, white, eye peering straight at Birch. Under the brightness of the laboratory lights, its pupil dilated to a pinpoint. It counted as the seventh out-of-place eye Birch had found since the first one appeared.

"How in holy hell do these things get in there?" McCormick said.

He stepped around the camera for a closer look. Lang leaned in from the other side. The soldiers inched in from the corners. Birch waved them back.

"Stay in position," Birch told them, and then to Lang, he said, "Bring a container."

Birch worked with the scalpel to remove the liver. The eye tracked the motions of his hand and the shining movements of the blade until the liver sliced free from the body. Then the eye blinked shut. Birch placed the dead organ in the container, set the specimen under a lamp on the counter, and studied it. Except for decay and the out-of-place eye, the liver appeared normal. He prodded it with the tip of a pen. The eye flinched but didn't open. Birch pressed the flesh around the eye; it gave like dried-up jelly in a balloon. The eye opened again, stark and expressionless. Birch made sure McCormick got a clear shot of it while he flashed a penlight into it and watched it follow the beam. Then he cut into the dead liver, excavating a space around the eye. The flesh came away in soft clumps. Birch exposed the entire eye, including a rudimentary optical nerve trailing from its anterior, buried in the meat, connected to nothing. After wiping off clinging bits of dead flesh, Birch placed the eye in a specimen jar and sealed it.

"How do you think they get there?" McCormick said.

"Indigestion," Lang said. "He ate someone who disagreed with him."

"You're joking, but you could be right," Birch said. "Dead limbs stay reanimated when they're separated from their body. Why not a dead eye after it's been devoured? Except look closely. It shows no signs of damage or decay. It wasn't chewed. And encysted in the liver like that? It's like it grew there."

"That couldn't happen, it growing there. That's not possible, right?" McCormick said. "Could that happen?"

"You still hung up on what's possible?" Birch said. "Thought we'd all gotten past wasting time on whether or not weird shit's possible. How is an eye growing inside a dead man's liver any harder to accept than the fact that the dead man in question is still moving and would take a bite out of any one of us if he could?"

Birch resumed dissecting the body. He removed half a dozen more organs before he found a second eye, this time embedded in a kidney. He, McCormick, and Lang repeated what they'd done with the liver and set the new eye beside the first one.

McCormick and Lang worked in silence after that. Birch sensed tension and fear in the soldiers. They'd crossed an unexpected threshold, stumbled upon something that made their nightmare a thousand times stranger and more frightening than only a few days ago, and Birch, in whom they'd entrusted all their hopes for an answer, couldn't yet explain it. Maybe he never would. Instead he kept dissecting the specimen, afraid that if he stopped, all of them in the room would crack up trying to make sense of something impossible to understand.

He found two more eyes before he finished.

After he cataloged and stored all the specimens, scrubbed the lab clean, and sent his assistants away, Birch uploaded a video clip of one of the eyes to the remnants of the Internet the government had protected. He posted it without comment as he had clips of the other anomalies he'd found in the last few days. He felt like a savage falling back on faith, casting a prayer into the ether, wishing for someone or something greater and wiser than himself to whisper back the truth in his ear.

DAY 27, 10:53 P.M.

Miniature stars of blood flickered in the air. Streaks of it whirled around Birch in the pattern of distant galaxies he had seen in pictures taken through powerful telescopes. He stood at the center of the swirling storm, desperate to keep clean and dry but failing as the blood spattered against him, a sideways rain, slicking him red. Wherever he moved, the vortex moved with him, its center locked on him, and both him and the storm trapped in a white, unfurnished room, a space lit by a gelid glow that emanated from its pristine walls.

Outside the room, people screamed.

Guns fired. A muted explosion erupted. Ground quaked.

Sticky fingers clutched at Birch's hand. Friedman had dragged himself across the floor, trailing broken legs and a double stripe of blood behind him. Strips of shredded, bloody cloth dangled where the dead had ripped through his clothes and gouged into his flesh. He was straining to reach Birch. Crimson bubbles danced on his lips as he tried to speak. Then his face twisted into a wretched expression, and he dropped and lay still.

The roar of the spinning blood rose until it drowned out the sounds of combat. Disoriented, Birch staggered around Friedman's corpse. An exit awaited on the far side of the room, a black rectangle cut into the shining, white wall. Fiery lightning-flashes lit it. Shapes moved through the darkness on the other side. Birch called out to them, but no one answered, or if someone did, the hissing storm of blood drowned it out.

Birch reached for the gun at his waist, but he wasn't wearing it. Almost too late, he remembered Friedman and turned back. The dead man was pulling himself along the floor toward him, moving faster than Birch would've expected. A kick to the head jolted Friedman onto his back, and then Birch bolted for the door. Crouching low, he fled the white room. As he entered the gloom outside, the spinning blood stilled, and the roar of the vortex died. All the blood dropped to the floor in a barrage of splashes.

Silence, now.

No gunshots or screams.

No muzzle flashes or explosions of light.

Gun smoke mixed with the stink of fresh blood, and the scorched scent of burning metal lingered in the air.

Behind Birch, the door to the white room blinked shut. Darkness crept in around him, leaving only a faint glow bobbing somewhere up ahead. Birch approached it, finding an electric lantern rolling like an egg on the floor. He didn't have to look far to see who'd dropped it. A soldier lay motionless up ahead, his hand reaching for the lantern handle. Lifting the light, Birch examined the dead man. His throat was torn out. Something blunt had been pounded into his chest, cracking his sternum, dragging bone and muscle with it when it was removed, leaving a gaping black cavity emptied of its heart. He read the name "Alvarez" stitched on the dead man's uniform but didn't know him.

He wandered, using the lantern to find his way. Its light drained into the shadows. Birch walked toward a steady plinking sound, tracking the noise down the rough, sloped floor of an earthen tunnel. The air swirled with a weak breeze rich with the scent of damp soil. Insects and vermin, invisible in the blackness, scuttled underfoot.

At the end of the tunnel, the lantern light touched a pair of booted feet swaying in the air. Birch inched forward, bearing the lantern like a shield. The light revealed another uniformed body, a familiar name stitched over the breast pocket. Birch hesitated. Sadness welled up in him, but he needed to know what held her up, why she danced and jerked in mid air. He lifted the lantern a few inches more. Two of the walking dead hung down like rats through the dirt ceiling of the tunnel roof, their gray, rotting hands buried deep in Private O'Neal's flesh, holding her close to their mouths so they could bite into her face and skull, into her neck and shoulders. They snarled at Birch, their rotting faces ripe with hunger. Their hair fell out in muddy clumps; maggots nested in what remained. The dead hissed at the light then continued feeding. Birch turned and ran, only to stumble hard and crash to the ground, smashing the lantern.

The dark came alive around him. He knew without seeing them that a ring of the dead tightened around him like the cables the soldiers used to herd the walking corpses. He wished for a weapon. He would've run back to O'Neal's body and taken her pistol, but he'd lost his sense of direction and had no idea where to go.

Then the darkness lifted. Everywhere Birch saw points of dull, white light like the afterimages of fireworks burned into his retinas. More blinked on each second. In the vast darkness Birch felt tiny and cold like a man adrift in space, surrounded by distant stars he could never reach, each one a sun that lit him with hatred as his life bled into the frigid vacuum. A faraway voice rumbled, deep and slow—calling to him.

He recognized it: the voice of the man in red.

Though distance muffled his words, his hatred and fury struck Birch like freezing water. Icy winds blew across his neck and face. He trembled from the cold.

The lights neared him, and he saw they weren't stars but eyes, thousands of pairs, peering out from the mist of a black corruption, their stares burning through him, making him feel like a ghost. Maybe that's all he was now, what all the living were in this world of the dead—remnants haunting a place to which they no longer belonged, a place that rejected them. The faraway voice came clearer: *You owe the dead everything. And they will take what is theirs.*

A door slammed shut with a sharp crash.

Real light returned.

Birch snapped upright and nearly toppled backward in his desk chair. He blinked against the harsh glow of the overhead fluorescents. He was in his lab. His back and neck ached with stiffness. McCormick and Lang, his assistants, busy at one of the tables, stopped work to stare at him.

"You okay?" Lang asked.

"What happened?" Birch said.

"You nodded off. We let you sleep. Figured you needed the rest."

Birch checked his watch. He had slept for twenty minutes.

"You're pale, man." McCormick held half a sandwich, munching on it while he worked. "Do you get any real sleep at all? I mean, fuck's sake, you need to take care of yourself. What if you'd nodded off like that while you were driving?"

"You idiot," Lang said. "Who drives anymore?"

Birch moved to the door. "I need some air. I'll be back."

Birch walked outside and tried not to think about what the dream meant, if it meant anything at all, if it wasn't only a nightmare born of stress and fear, if the man in red wasn't only a creation of his subconscious terror. Birch found the pressure harder to bear every day. The shit rolled downhill harder from Novak, who was being pressed for results by General Collier, who in turn was sweating it with his boss and the president, but Birch had little more to offer them. Everything he learned about the strange bacterium was measured and analyzed, and still all Birch's data divulged no secret. Standard tetanus treatments didn't affect the bacteria strain, and every new approach he conceived proved useless. He had been unable to come up with any explanation for eyes found inside the corpses, and that seemed to bother Novak more than anything else. They'd already stayed at Vanguard a week longer than they should've. Their isolation no longer protected them as much as it had. The dead were getting harder to manage and more numerous. Soldiers ran "wrap and smash" ops four or five times a day. They put their lives at risk so Birch could keep working in the best facility possible.

They held out so he could stop the dead from walking.

Except he no longer believed he could, at least not by any means discoverable in a laboratory. He could devise no scientific explanation for why the dead returned to activity nor any meaning for the eyes embedded in their corrupt flesh. The face and voice of the man in red haunted him, inescapable, inevitable, a glaring reminder of his failure, a sign of what Birch suspected was the immutable truth—that the dead couldn't be stopped by the living.

The tide of nature had turned to favor them, forcing the living to run and hide, but for those at Vanguard, it was too late even for that. Leaving for a more secure location now would be a bitter pill, not only for Birch's failure, but because Birch knew people would die on the way, lives sacrificed to buy him extra time that had led nowhere.

He crossed the big lawn toward the main entrance, aiming for the bright dots of a night patrol's flashlights. Too much light attracted the dead, so they kept the parking lot street lamps dark and avoided using spotlights. Ahead of him, Birch saw a cluster of little lights indicating soldiers gathered near the dense hedge that edged the parking lot.

He veered for it then halted when a feathered slash of fire streaked the night, igniting a body Birch hadn't seen in the dark. The burning corpse shuffled in circles for several seconds before it collapsed. A second blast of flame touched it. Birch waited for others to show. Remembering his latest dream, he touched the gun at his hip and found its cold presence reassuring. Only the crackle of flames disturbed the night quiet, not moans from any other nearby dead. When the corpse burned long enough, the soldiers hosed it down, spewing up a cloud of gray smoke. Birch approached as they began to beat the charred remains with axes and iron pipes, breaking it to pieces.

One of the soldiers, with a pair of night vision lenses hanging from his neck, met Birch and waved him back. "Sir, you shouldn't be out here."

"Yeah, tell me about it, but I had to get out of that lab and get some air before I snapped," Birch said.

The soldier lifted his flashlight, briefly blinding Birch, then lowered it to paint Birch's ID badge hanging from a lanyard. "Sorry, Dr. Birch. Didn't realize it was you."

"No problem. Lot of them coming in?"

"Thirteenth one tonight. It's more than last week, sir, and a hell of a lot more than the week before. We get a lot more coming in groups now, too. Hard to spot them at night, they're so damn quiet sometimes. Infrared is useless, but we can see them with our night eyes. I don't know if they can talk to each other, but if they can I'd say word's out that we're the graveyard hotspot. Anyone who's anyone who's dead wants in here."

Birch nodded. "Or it could be there's so many dead now, they're spreading everywhere in larger numbers."

"Thanks for that depressing alternative, sir."

"Sorry," Birch said. "Private O'Neal on duty tonight?"

"Checkpoint Echo, sir. You heading over there?"

"Yeah. Echo's the west gate?"

"Yes, sir. I'll radio over, let them know you're coming," The soldier handed Birch a flashlight from his belt. "Take my backup. You'll need it."

"Thanks." Birch clicked on the light. The beam lit up the name stitched across the soldier's shirt: Alvarez.

Birch spoke the name without thinking.

"Yes, sir?" Alvarez said.

Birch couldn't reply. Bloody, dream images of Alvarez flashed back to him, transposed over the man standing before him. Birch couldn't remember ever meeting Alvarez before tonight, yet in his dream he'd known exactly what he looked like, even down to the way the man wore his uniform.

"Sir?" Alvarez asked.

"You're Sergeant Alvarez. We haven't met before."

"No, sir," Alvarez said. "Is something wrong?"

"No. Major Novak speaks highly of you. That's all. It's good to meet you."

"Good to meet you, too. I'll radio Echo, now."

Birch crossed the open lawn toward the west gate. Halfway there, he realized that with so little light from the normally bright complex, hundreds, if not thousands, more stars occupied the night sky. Their light fell on his face. He felt naked and exposed. Vulnerable. Thoughts of swirling blood and constellations of eyes and a voice that spoke to him from the void came to mind. He kept his fingers crossed that O'Neal would have a little time to talk. She was a good listener. He hoped he'd be able to put the dream image of her dead out of his mind while he was with her.

He knew he wouldn't.

DAY 35, 11:37 A.M.

Birch embraced O'Neal then kissed her, but she pushed him away and backed against the wall. Puzzled, Birch sat down on the bed. O'Neal held a manila envelope in her right hand. She and Birch hid out in the storeroom where she'd convalesced; they'd been using it to slip away together. The stench that had clung to the room weeks ago lingered no more. Dickie Stein's corpse next door had decomposed past the point of stinking, and Birch's living dead specimens down the hall had hardened into a state of arrested decay. No one upstairs remembered they'd put a bed down here. O'Neal usually showed up for their rendezvous smiling and bright, happy to lock the door behind them and shut out the awful world for awhile. In only the past few days, though, the number of dead wandering into the Vanguard complex had doubled, putting everyone on edge. Still, O'Neal seemed more shaken now than Birch had seen her since she'd been wounded by the dead.

"What's in the envelope?" he asked.

"Photos."

Birch held out his hand. "Let me see."

O'Neal held them back. "You don't have clearance—but I think I'm supposed to give them to you anyway."

"What do you mean?"

O'Neal frowned. She crossed the room, sat beside Birch on the bed, and leaned her head on his shoulder. "We knew it wouldn't last. You knew that, right? This thing we have, our escape? It's been fantastic. You've been fantastic. With everything falling apart and dying, I never thought there could be anything like what we have. But it couldn't last, could it?"

"What, are you dumping me?" Birch said, and then he laughed. "Or are you pulling out? Did Collier change your orders?"

"No. Orders are to stay put, hold the complex, keep you online working. They're desperate, and they won't let go. They figure you have the best chance of success here with your equipment."

"Then, what is it?"

The way O'Neal shuddered against him made the room feel cold like a cell, and for a moment, Birch thought of himself as trapped, a prisoner. Then he took the envelope from O'Neal's hand. She let him.

"Major Novak called me into his office this morning to review patrol schedules. That was bullshit. All he talked about was you. He knows about our affair, but he doesn't care. He thinks you're our best hope of ending the dead plague, so whatever it takes to keep you happy, keep you functioning is worthwhile, including me. I was insulted at first, but then I realized he meant we have to protect you. We have to keep you going until you find the answer."

"I'm not sure it's there to be found," Birch said.

"Novak got up and went to get coffee. Took almost ten minutes to do it, and he left what's in that envelope out on his desk in the open, where he knew I'd see them. He *wanted* me to see them. I *think* he wanted me to take them. After I saw them I couldn't do anything else. When Novak came back, he acted like he didn't even notice they were gone. I'm supposed to warn you. Look."

Birch slid out a handful of 8 ½ x 11 pictures printed on glossy photo paper and spread them out on his lap. Dated between 12 and 14 hours ago, satellite images of the Vanguard complex and its vicinity showed crowds of walking dead flooding the land like an invading army fifteen to twenty miles northeast of the complex. The sequence of images illustrated them moving closer. Birch examined the pictures twice. In eighteen to twenty hours the dead would overrun the Vanguard complex. Birch's fingers brushed a slip of paper taped to the back of the most recent image, a note scrawled in Novak's handwriting: "Take your equipment and whomever you need. I'll leave you a van and weapons by the south exit. Head out before dawn."

"I didn't see that before." O'Neal read the note and let out a long breath. "I was afraid I'd screwed up."

"Collier and the others know we can't survive this." Birch stood and paced the room. "They have to know. But they're keeping us here anyway."

"Maybe they don't know what else to do."

"We leave. Hide somewhere else."

"You told them there's no place with equipment as good as what you have here."

"It's worthless. I won't find the answers in my lab. It's something beyond that."

"Maybe they think Novak's men can protect us."

"Are you kidding?"

"These guys are sitting it out in a bunker somewhere. You think General Collier's ever worked 'wrap and smash' duty? Bastard probably hasn't ever come within three feet of one of the rotters, probably hasn't ever even smelled one."

"We should warn everyone. Get them all out of here."

"No. You'll force Novak to stop us. He won't disobey orders. He won't run from a fight, even if he can't win."

Birch wanted to argue that reason and common sense would prevail, but then he remembered Novak's rant about his first cup of coffee in the morning. Some boundaries the major wouldn't break. He would follow orders to his last breath.

"Why is he giving me an out?" Birch said.

"He believes you can end the dead plague," O'Neal said. "And he knows losing you will cost us our best chance. Maybe, he doesn't want to risk that. If I were a betting woman, I'd wager Collier ordered him to protect you to the best of his ability, not keep you prisoner. There's enough wiggle room there even for Novak to rationalize warning you."

"I guess. But, Joan, if there's a solution, it's outside my capabilities to discover it." Birch wished he felt the clarity of purpose he saw in O'Neal's eyes. " I don't mean it's too advanced. I mean it's unscientific. They don't need a biologist to figure this out, they need a, a...fucking magician, or a theologian."

O'Neal's expression soured. "Don't give me that cop-out bullshit. You got further than anyone else. There were others working on this. No one got into it as deeply as you did." O'Neal held Birch's hand. "It's only a matter of time. Something hasn't occurred to you yet, you haven't found all the information you need. Even if you're right, so what? You want to die here and become one of those things? Novak's giving you an escape. Don't squander it."

"Everyone left behind will die."

"Maybe not. They're good fighters."

Birch pushed the photos into O'Neal's hands.

"They are. They're the best. But there aren't enough of them for *this*. Not by a fucking long shot. Ammo is low. They won't last a day."

O'Neal scowled and tossed the pictures to the floor. "Figure out what you need and who should go."

"You. I need you," Birch said. "Come with me."

"Are you sure?"

"I won't leave you behind. I won't forget you."

"Okay," O'Neal said. She drew Birch down onto the bed beside her. "But first, because who knows when we'll have another chance to be alone like this...."

Birch slipped his arms around O'Neal and held her. He tried to mask his anxiety, but he knew she could feel it, even as he felt how badly she wanted to ease it, to make him see things in the same clear-cut way she did. Her touch drove some of the tension from his body. She gave him the last light in a dying world. He wouldn't let go of her; if he had to flee the dead and abandon the living to stay with her then he would.

DAY 36, 1:07, A.M.

Every night between 12 a.m. and 5 a.m., the labs closed and all nonessential equipment powered down to conserve generator fuel. The research crews bunked in an ancillary building and half a dozen field tents that Novak's men had pitched on the back lawn, leaving the main facility empty. The corridors of the lab center stretched into a fragile stillness. Birch and Sergeant Alvarez found their way through it by flashlight, Birch still using the one Alvarez had given him the night he'd first dreamt of the soldier's death—and O'Neal's.

Similar dreams had come to Birch many times in the past weeks, all of them brutal and disturbing. Alvarez, Friedman, and O'Neal appeared in some of them, dead or dying, or even as one of the walking dead, mindless and ugly. So Birch had decided to take them all with him when he left, hoping to spare them from the dead horde, and maybe save their lives. Others had appeared in his dreams too. Lang and McCormick, Private Nelson and Private Robbins who'd made chopper runs to the hospital with him, all of them doomed in his visions. He wanted to take them all. Assuming his dreams were premonitions, perhaps he could save their lives. If he kept them nearby, maybe he could protect them. Maybe not. But anyone who stayed behind would certainly die. Sometimes, the dreams were only jumbles of faces and bodies, men and women with guns, children, soldiers, moving through a landscape jammed with rippling, infinite crowds of the living and the dead. Always, Birch heard the voice of the man in red, low, deep, and muffled, like the hum of a distant machine. But it was growing louder. Coming nearer as if the dead pressed harder against Birch's consciousness the closer they came to the Vanguard complex.

Alvarez stopped at the door to Birch's lab. Birch tried not to look at his face. When he did, he only saw his dream vision of it, broken and bloodied, haunted by the frozen stare of its dead eyes. Birch unlocked the door. Alvarez pushed it open and washed the room with light.

"Clear, sir," he said.

Birch entered and walked to his desk. He unplugged his laptop, coiled up the charger, slid it into a case, and placed it on a table by the door. He took two empty boxes from the closet and set them beside it, then he gathered items from the lab and packed them. He took four more laptops, along with a stack of notebooks, and a thick, fanfold spreadsheet printout. He gathered up test tubes, microscope slides, and ampoules, then packed them in and padded them with scrap paper pulled from the trash bin. Alvarez monitored the corridor, but no one came. They heard only the faint voices of the night patrol calling as they lit up the latest dead arrival at the perimeter. Birch slung three of the laptops from his shoulders and picked up one of the boxes. Alvarez took the other box and the remaining two computers.

"I want some things from Friedman's lab," Birch said.

They walked to a lab at the far end of the corridor. Friedman's space stank of formaldehyde. A chemist, he worked on ways to accelerate physical decomposition, trying to create a powder or spray to turn the walking dead into instant rot. Birch found another box and placed two microscopes into it then took Friedman's laptop and another one, splitting them up between him and Alvarez. He stacked the new box on top of the first one and let Alvarez lead the way. The men strained from the load they carried.

"Can I ask you a question, sir?" Alvarez said.

"Shoot."

"Why me? Private O'Neal told me how Novak warned you and all, but I don't see why you picked me. You could've taken anyone. You hardly know me."

"I trust you," Birch said, afraid to admit the real reason. "You gave me your flashlight."

"That's it?"

"Isn't that enough? I had to pick someone."

"If you say so, sir."

They turned down another long hallway and followed it to a side exit that came out away from the front parking lot and the tents at the rear. The van stood fifty yards away across the grass, parked at the end of an access road that led to a small equipment shed and vehicle area used by Vanguard's maintenance crew. A dirt trail beyond the shed led to a back road that connected with the highway five miles south. Birch had sometimes used the route as a shortcut home. He and Alvarez loaded the boxes and computers into the truck.

"Seems like not much to take, sir," said Alvarez.

"It'll do. The really powerful stuff is too big or too sensitive to move. Let's go round up O'Neal and the others."

Birch and Alvarez headed for the tents, careful to stay quiet. O'Neal had already gone to rouse Friedman and enlist his help in gathering the rest of the group. She was to make everything sound like an order from Major Novak so no one would argue much about being woken in the middle of the night. Three figures emerged from one of the tents. Birch whistled. The trio stopped and waited for Birch and Alvarez to catch up to them—O'Neal, Friedman, and Lang, the latter two clutching backpacks and briefcases.

"Birch!" Friedman looked disheveled and worried. "What the hell's happening?"

"No time to explain, Carl," Birch said. "We need Robbins, McCormick, and Nelson, fast as we can find them."

"Is the perimeter breached?"

Birch said, "Not yet."

The group crept past the darkened tents, stopping at two more, while Private O'Neal went in to wake the last three people. Packed with equipment and baggage, the small van could hold eight. Birch had chosen his list from his best researchers and those he'd seen most often in his dreams. He wanted to take so many others, people he'd worked with every day for years, people he trusted, people who deserved better than the fate he was leaving them to. But really everyone deserved better than that, and for those left behind, their end would be no different than that of almost everyone else in the world. On the road, his band of refugees could wind up dead before they reached the highway for all he knew.

At the van, Private O'Neal opened the doors. Friedman spotted his computer and lab samples.

"You raided my lab?" he said. "This has gone too far! No doubt I speak for all here when I say there's no way in hell I'm getting in this van until you explain what the fuck is going on."

"We're relocating," Birch said. "Novak's orders."

"Stealing away in the middle of the night? With research and equipment that legally belongs either to the Vanguard Corporation or the U.S. Army? You'll have to lie better than that."

Most of the group stood around Friedman, their curious expressions angled at Birch, all of them weary and sallow in the van's weak light. Only O'Neal and Alvarez stood with Birch. They were armed, and Birch knew they'd comply if he asked them to force the others into the vehicle. Instead he reached into the van and pulled the envelope of satellite photos from one of the boxes. He passed around the pictures, told how O'Neal had gotten them, embellishing as if Novak was as eager to save Friedman as he was Birch. If Birch could win Friedman's support, he'd help him convince the others.

Birch waited while it sank in. He watched the black horizon, the shadowed squares of the Vanguard building, the faint lights of the night patrols. He smelled burning flesh and hair and knew another dead invader had been eliminated. An aroma of decay came on the breeze. It hadn't been there yesterday, and Birch thought how close the huge march of the dead must be by now. His hand shook. He willed it steady, but it didn't work.

Friedman touched his shoulder. Birch saw a fresh, wet redness in the man's eyes.

"God damn it," Friedman said. "God damn the dead."

The others were already boarding the van.

Alvarez, behind the wheel, started up the engine. Birch nodded at Friedman, took the photos, and the two men got in the van. Friedman squeezed into the back. Birch took the passenger seat beside O'Neal, who sat in the middle. The last door shut. Alvarez pulled out, waiting until they'd rounded a bend in the road before he switched on the headlights. In the woods, the light did little to cut the dark. A minute later they passed the shed. The smooth road ended, and the van jolted over rough dirt. Birch watched clear sky dappled with stars roll past above jagged tree shadows. O'Neal held his hand. The van jolted, slamming its passengers together. Something glass shattered in one of the boxes.

"Shit," McCormick said. "I hope that wasn't anything contagious."

"You idiot," Lang said.

The ride smoothed out. A black road stretched into the darkness. Birch focused on the broken white line down its middle and watched the van devour it.

DAY 36, 1:12 P.M.

Birch snapped awake with sun in his eyes. He had fallen asleep around dawn, while Alvarez picked a slow route along a highway littered with abandoned vehicles. The motion had settled Birch, allowing exhaustion to overtake him. He didn't feel rested for having slept, though, only achy and dried out. His head throbbed.

"Why did we stop?" he said.

He reached for O'Neal, but she wasn't there.

"Bathroom break." Alvarez reclined in the driver's seat, hands behind his head. "We didn't want to wake you."

Birch straightened himself. The others were standing in front of the van, talking and stretching. O'Neal appeared from the thick brush at the side of the road, buckling her belt as she emerged. The van sat parked on the shoulder above a pit dotted with mounds of dirt, sand, and lime, and gouged with shallow trenches. There were no cars around. A bulldozer and a digger occupied the pit's far side along with a steamroller. Construction equipment lay scattered around them. Stuck to the ground at the center of the pit, a scrap of white cloth fluttered in the breeze. The edge of a golf course was visible through the trees. Farther up the shoulder sat a trailer, its windows smashed, its door hanging from one hinge. A lopsided sign beside it announced a building project, but only the words "Coming Soon" and the torn, faded picture of a clubhouse remained visible. The grass and weeds around the trailer lay trampled flat, a web of tire tracks sculpted in the dried mud. Beyond it, the road—a two-lane strip of cracked pavement— curved around a bend and vanished into dense woods.

"Why are we off the highway?" Birch said. He reached into the back of the van, took a bottle of water, and drank most of it.

"About an hour after you crashed, it got impassable," Alvarez told him. "Cars and trucks jammed up everywhere. Clusters of the dead got thicker. Some were hiding in the cars. We couldn't go any farther. Had to find another way. We're kind of making it up as we go along now, but the driving's been smooth. We've been traveling south. Put about 300 miles between us and Vanguard. We'll need gas soon. I've already used one of our spare cans."

"Okay," Birch said. "We'll take care of it."

"The map shows a town a few miles down the road. Chances are we can fuel up there."

"Good."

"Sooner or later," Alvarez said, "we have to decide where we're going."

"We will," Birch said. "One thing at a time."

He stepped out of the van and blinked at the daylight. O'Neal came and hugged him, and Birch kissed her. It felt good to hold her in the open air and the warmth of the sun.

"We made it," she said.

Birch took a head count. No one missing.

"So far, so good," he said.

Birch walked to the bushes to relieve himself. When he finished and turned back toward the van, the sun caught his eyes and filled his sight with a hazy whiteness. The light flared magnesium bright and stabbed through his skull. Sharp pain blossomed in his head and throbbed with a frantic beat. An unwelcome murmur filled his thoughts: the voice of the man in red. Birch didn't understand the words, but the voice called to him. He felt made of paper and air, like he might float away on the breeze or catch fire and burn in an instant. The world spun. He dropped to his knees, tilted sideways to the ground, which seemed ephemeral, as if he would pass right through it, and fell. O'Neal shouted, her voice dim, faraway. Birch glimpsed the others rushing toward him, shimmering like mirages in a burning whiteness that saturated the world.

Then they were gone.

A whooshing roar rose in Birch's head, blood pulsing through his arteries like a rushing river.

Whiteness surrounded him.

Nothing beneath his body.

He floated.

Black specks broke the whiteness.

The specks blinked.

Eyes.

They stared at Birch, a negative of his dream of drifting in space surrounded by constellations of eyes. Birch tried to touch them, but they blinked away. The man in red's voice grew louder, clearer, as if it came from everywhere.

Don't fear this new world. I'll protect you. In the end, you'll be at my side. I'll make sure of it. You are my witness, but only you, and you alone.

The pain in Birch's head spiked.

He moaned and rolled over, sensing the ground beneath him again; grass folded under his hands and rocks bit into his back. Blue sky and swaying green leaves replaced the white light. Birch glimpsed flashes of motion. He heard gunfire and shouting. O'Neal screamed. Someone was crying. Birch dragged himself onto his knees. The man in red stood over him, staring into Birch's face with a pallid expression that mingled hatred, anger, and sorrow. Birch stared into the dead man's face, his mind aching to recall it but producing only the vague resonance of a memory. Red rags fluttered on the dead man's body. Fresh blood ran down his hands. He touched Birch's forehead with one finger and smeared blood there.

"No!" O'Neal shouted. "Get away from him!"

O'Neal fired her gun. Bullets slashed the air, but the dead man in red disappeared.

O'Neal saw him touching me. O'Neal saw him. *He was really here, and he touched me.*

O'Neal hefted Birch onto his feet and pulled him toward the van. The dead were everywhere, and the rest of Birch's crew was already dead or fighting for their lives.

Birch struggled to clear his head. He leaned against the van and pulled his gun.

The dead poured out of the nearby woods. They rose from shallow trenches in the pit, where they'd been buried under layers of lime and sand. It dawned on Birch that what had been a construction site had been converted to a burial ground, probably in the early days of the dead plague before anyone realized how useless it was to bury the walking dead. With no living people to draw them out, the dead had simply waited beneath the sand and soil. And Birch's refugees had roused them. Corpses surrounded the van and drew the circle tighter around them. *Wrap and smash.* Robbins and Nelson lay facedown in the road. The dead dragged them over the pavement, pulling them apart piece by piece and eating them. Lang ran across the pit, dodging walking corpses, nowhere for him to go. More of the things spilled out of the woods and clambered up from the shallow mass graves. Birch heard McCormick, who'd climbed up a tree to escape, crying. Part of his intestines hung down from a bloody wound in his stomach. The dead tugged on it even as McCormick tried to gather it up and shove it back inside his abdomen. Only Alvarez and Friedman remained in the clear, hunkered along the front of the van, firing round after round into the approaching wall of corpses.

"Get in the van!" O'Neal shouted.

She shoved Birch through the open side door then climbed in after him and yanked it closed. Alvarez and Friedman worked their way along opposite sides of the van; Alvarez scrambled into the driver's seat and Friedman the passenger's. The motor revved. The van jolted as Alvarez floored the gas and drove into the line of the dead. The van thumped into body after body, knocking them aside, grinding them under its wheels, but there were too many. The dead piled up, and their bodies jammed the tires and stuck to the chassis. The van shuddered then skidded sideways before it stopped.

Alvarez pumped the gas, but the vehicle's wheels only spun in dead flesh like soft mud. Dead fists pounded on the doors, on the windows.

The passenger side window shattered, spraying cubes of glass onto Friedman. Half a dozen hands thrust through the opening and grabbed his head. On the driver's side, the door cracked ajar. Alvarez fought to close it, but the weight of the dead over-powered him. Gray, rotting hands reached through the cracks and pried the door open wider. Birch and O'Neal crab-walked to the back of the van. O'Neal reloaded her gun.

Alvarez's grip on the door slid loose, and it sprang back, exposing him. A mob of writhing, grabbing dead bodies with black mouths stretched wide swallowed him up.

Friedman screamed as the dead ripped away his hair and part of his scalp. He shoved his gun through the window and fired until it was empty. Five shots. The reports exploded inside the van, almost deafening Birch. He barely heard Friedman's shrieks when the dead forced the passenger side door open and dragged him away.

He looked at O'Neal. She clutched her gun and stared at the rotten, gray faces pressed against the windshield. She was braced to fight, her face slick with sweat, her chest heaving as she breathed. The dead climbed in through the front doors.

"Come on," Birch said.

He grabbed O'Neal's arm and pulled her to the side door, threw it open, and leapt to the ground. The dead were thin there, most of them drawn to the fresh bodies on the ground by the front of the van. Birch didn't think he and O'Neal could escape, but he preferred to go down running and fighting rather than trapped in the back of the van. He wanted to see blue sky and sun and green leaves dancing in the wind as he died. With O'Neal close behind him, he picked a path through the gray crowd. The only way led down to the pit, where more of the dead waited. Birch spied the empty golf course beyond and thought if they made it there, they might have a chance.

In the pit, the sand slowed them down. Birch twisted and weaved to avoid dead hands that grabbed for them. The dead seemed lethargic even for corpses. Some of them even staggered away from Birch as he neared—as if avoiding him. Birch wondered why, but he didn't care if it meant he and O'Neal would reach the far side of the pit.

Then O'Neal screamed.

Her hand jerked free from Birch's.

Birch slid to a stop and turned back, only to face a wall of the dead gathered behind him; they swarmed over O'Neal, taking her away.

Birch threw himself into the dead, pushing, fighting, digging his way past them, but there were too many. He couldn't shove through them. They no longer moved out of his way. O'Neal screamed. Her voice cut Birch to his soul. He glimpsed her face, saw her fists flying, feet kicking, but dozens of the dead fell onto her, scrabbling for a piece of her. Through a gap in the crowd, Birch glimpsed a flash of red, and then the hole closed.

A dead hand waved past his face; an eye stared out from its palm.

From the back of one of the dead, three eyes blinked open and looked at Birch.

Eyes appeared on the legs of one corpse, in the cheeks and forehead of another, on the chest of a third.

Wherever the dead eyes blinked open, they turned toward Birch and burned him with their stare. Even as the dead wandered the pit or fought over the scraps of Alvarez, Friedman, and the others, the harsh, angry eyes that popped open on their rotting bodies locked on Birch. It was horrible to be seen by them. Birch tried again to reach O'Neal. He couldn't get past the dead. Then O'Neal's screams stopped. Birch dropped to his knees in the sand and waited for the dead to take him.

They didn't.

They moved around him like he wasn't there.

Like he was one of them.

Birch rejected that. He was alive.

He was still alive.

He stood and walked into the densest throngs of the dead. They stepped aside; they ignored him when he hit them. When he grabbed one, shoved him to the ground, and kicked him, the dead thing only rolled over and worked to get back on his feet.

"You've killed everyone else," Birch screamed. "Why won't you kill me?"

The dead didn't answer.

A hand fell on Birch's shoulder.

He whirled around.

O'Neal.

Her face was ashen and blank, a ravenous slate. Blood smeared her torn uniform. Her throat had been ripped out, and all over her body were fresh cuts and gouges, where the dead had eaten bits of her. Her hair was matted with sand and gore. Her lips moved but no words came. Birch reached to touch her then snatched his hand back. He didn't want to feel her cold, dead skin. This wasn't O'Neal any more, wasn't anything he'd ever loved or cared about; it wasn't anything human.

O'Neal shuffled closer.

She opened her mouth. Hunger filled her eyes. Her gaze seemed to cast out past Birch, who was invisible to her now, her dead stare seeking some unattainable, faraway thing beyond the horizon, beyond the world.

Then O'Neal's eyes rolled back in their sockets. Her body collapsed, and she dropped to the sand, where she lay dead still.

The man in red stood behind her, his hand lingering where he'd touched O'Neal.

Birch flinched at the sight of him.

I give her the gift you cannot. In the end it will be only you and you alone.

The man in red vanished.

Birch knelt beside O'Neal's body and stared at the sky. It was the same as it ever was, and that seemed utterly wrong. Three sparrows glided by, circled, and then flew into the shadows of the trees.

Birch wept.

DAY 36, 3:27 P.M.

Only you.
And you alone.

Birch wiped his face and stood. The dead thinned out and scattered into the woods or along the road. Clusters of them lingered over the bodies of Birch's fallen friends. All of them but O'Neal had reanimated, their bodies so damaged they would never get up and walk.

Birch returned to the van, and as he cleared the stuck bodies from the wheels and the bumpers, not one of them tried to bite or grab him. When he finished freeing the van, Birch got in and started the engine. A second later he shut it off. He left the van, walked across the pit, and took a shovel from the equipment near the construction machines. He chose a place on the edge of the woods, a patch of ground beneath three tall oaks, and he dug. His body protested the effort with aches and pains, but Birch ignored them. When he was done, he took O'Neal's body in his arms, carried her to the grave, and buried her. It was twilight when he emptied the last shovelful of dirt onto her.

He thought he should say something, but he could barely think or feel anymore and only "Don't Panic" came to mind so he left her in silence.

Back in the van, he glimpsed himself in the rearview mirror and saw a man crusted with sand and dirt and gore and drying sweat. Deep red, almost black on his forehead glistened the smear of blood the dead man in red had put there.

That was why the dead wouldn't touch me. I've been marked, claimed, and god help me whatever that means.

Birch glanced at the fuel gauge and remembered Alvarez's warning about filling up with gas in the next town. Then he drove down the road, hoping to escape something he could never outrun.

ESCAPE FROM THE PRISON OF THE BLIND DEAD 21ST-CENTURY REDUX

THE ORIGINS OF CORPSE FAUNA

The Corpse Fauna story cycle was born in 1997, but it's taken more than a few years (a couple of decades now as of this edition) for it to grow up and come into its own. That year was a big, chaotic year for me. I quit a job editing comic books in Florida, moved home to New York, found a new job, got married, moved again, launched an independent comic book series, *Shadow House*, with writer Christopher Mills, and settled in to get serious about writing prose fiction. Looking back, it's a miracle I survived. It's only the resilience of youth that allowed me to take on all the stress, sleep deprivation, and surprises that year brought me; it's only the ignorance of youth that made me confident enough to take all the *risks* involved with doing those things. Which isn't to say I wouldn't do it all over again because I certainly would. Yet even with all that going on, I had other ambitions in the works.

One of those was a comic book project to follow up *Shadow House.*

A one-shot titled, *Zombie Hell.*

The idea was Chris's, but it was born at least in part from the many conversations we'd had about our love for zombie* fiction in all its forms. At that time, that meant primarily George Romero's classic dead movies, Skipp and Spector's *Book of the Dead* anthologies, and the comic book series, *Deadworld*. This was before Zak Snyder remade *Dawn of the Dead*, before Romero returned to the *Land of the Dead*, before *The Walking Dead* became a hit comic and television show, before even the influence of Brian Keene's landmark novel, The Rising, was fully known. Today, even the Centers for Disease Control are in on the action, using the zombie apocalypse in public service announcements about disaster preparedness.

Chris and I had no idea in 1997 how timely the idea for *Zombie Hell* was.

Who can say what might have been if we'd followed through and published it?

Possibly, there would be no Corpse Fauna series today. That's because the germ of what has become Corpse Fauna was in one of the stories I would've written for *Zombie Hell*. It would've been an eight- or ten-page story about an old-timer in prison when the zombie apocalypse occurs, an old-timer due to get out of prison in only a few weeks, but who sees his last chance for freedom vanish into the mouths of the hungry hordes of the living dead.

Sadly, it was not to be.

Shadow House proved to be a critical success but not a commercial one. The artwork was stellar, created by Dan Brereton, Pat Broderick, John Estes, Fred Harper, Art Nichols, and Kirk Van Wormer, all of whom graced the book with their spectacular talents. The book received good reviews and great comments from people like Brian Michael Bendis, Barry Lyga, and William F. Nolan. But even with those things in our corner and strong support from Diamond Distribution, *Shadow House* never quite broke the sales threshold necessary to keep it alive.

---

*I recognize the distinction between a true, traditional zombie and the walking dead, a line that has become thoroughly blurred in popular culture. For convenience's sake, I refer to the walking dead as zombies in this afterword, but they are not called zombies in the *Corpse Fauna* stories, and I don't consider them true zombies. In my mind, they are, simply, the dead, and they owe much more to George Romero and Dan O'Bannon than to Papa Legba and Baron Cemeterie.

In other words, Chris and I were going deeper into debt with each issue, and orders—though rising—weren't rising fast enough. Then logistical and personal issues weighed in and made it more and more difficult to produce each issue.

Shadow House ended with issue five, one issue shy of completing our first story lines, two issues shy of the single-issue epic crossover Chris and I had planned for issue seven.

With the demise of *Shadow House*, the idea for *Zombie Hell*—and a few other projects Chris and I were planning—were consigned the morgue of dead concepts.

THE DEAD RESURRECTED

The morgue is where my "old-timer in prison" zombie story might have stayed if not for Vince Sneed. Vince and I had met through comics. Vince liked *Shadow House.* I liked Vince's comic *Forty Winks*, drawn by John Peters. It didn't take long for me and Vince to figure out we had a lot of common interests in comics, literature, and movies—including zombies. We got to talking, and sometime in 2001 (I don't recall the exact date), Vince asked me a fateful question. He'd gotten a hankering to do some publishing and was looking for some fun material for his first chapbook. He asked me, "You got any ideas for a zombie story?"

"Actually, yes," I said. "I've got this idea for a thing with zombies in prison."

By the end of the conversation, the chapbook was planned. Vince was calling it "Prison of the Blind Dead" (mostly, I think because the infamous Blind Dead movies had recently been released on DVD and Vince had blind zombies on the brain). He even sent me a logo design for the title only a few days later. As I commenced writing, my comic book short story evolved into a much longer prose piece, and the old-timer faded into the background in favor of a new character, Cornell. The old-timer, Old Corntooth, is still there, still largely the way I originally envisioned him, and unless you're reading this Afterword before you read the novella, you've already met him—and you know the story simply outgrew him.

I sent Vince the manuscript with a new title, "The Dead Bear Witness."

Vince (begrudgingly) agreed to the title change and in 2002, the story was published by Die, Monster, Die Books, the inaugural publication of Vince's new publishing venture. It featured a wonderfully lurid cover illustration by Kirk Van Wormer and an interior illustration by Carla Speed McNeil. "The Dead Bear Witness" helped pave the way for Vince's first book project, *The Dead Walk!* (2004), an anthology of zombie stories. That book reprinted "The Dead Bear Witness" and included another of my zombie stories, "Resurrection House." By small press standards, it was a hit, and if you were at the Horrorfind Weekend in 2004, chances are you remember the surfing zombie T-shirt that promoted the book with the caption: "Zombie summer would never end."

Die, Monster, Die went on to publish several more anthologies, novellas, and novels. Vince edited a follow-up anthology, *The Dead Walk Again!* (2007), published by Padwolf Publishing, which included the next major Corpse Fauna story, "The Dead in their Masses." An early version of a third Corpse Fauna story, "Crying Tears of Blood, Sweet like Honey," appeared in *Bare Bone*, issue nine, in 2006, edited by Kevin L. Donihe and published by Raw Dog Screaming Press.

Not bad for a story idea that once seemed doomed to the dustbin of creative dreams.

The long con for all this was a meaty collection of all the Corpse Fauna stories in definitive, expanded versions, with new material in a single volume that would complete the Corpse Fauna story cycle. It was to be published by Die, Monster, Die Books.

As with *Shadow House*, though, an array of intruding realities led to the end of DMD before that book was realized. Corpse Fauna once again found itself on the slab.

THE DEAD WON'T DIE

Enter Dark Quest Books.

Many Balticons ago, publisher Neal Levin and I were talking about how e-books were changing the nature of publishing, opening new opportunities, keeping authors and publishers on their toes, and generally shaking things up. Neal mentioned he liked publishing novellas, and in short order I proposed publishing the complete Corpse Fauna stories as a series of expanded novellas with additional short stories. Discussion ensued, a formal proposal was presented, Neal agreed, and Corpse Fauna returned to stalk the living.

That incarnation of the series included some previously published material, all of which was revised, refined, and greatly expanded. The version of "The Dead Bear Witness" published in the first Dark Quest volume, for example, was more than double the length of the original story, fleshed out with greater characterization, a deeper look into the Corpse Fauna world, and a little added weirdness. "Birch's Refugees" was published there for the first time.

I realized working on Corpse Fauna again that the world had changed since "The Dead Bear Witness" was first published. That posed one of the biggest challenges in preparing these stories for fresh publication. Given how much zombie fiction has been published and how many zombie movies were released in the past decade was Corpse Fauna still relevant?

Corpse Fauna has its roots firmly planted in the territory blazed by George Romero, Lucio Fulci, Skipp and Spector, Stuart Kerr and Vince Locke, but in many ways the state of zombie fiction has moved beyond that. The basic survival story that shaped many a classic tale of the zombie apocalypse has been retold to near exhaustion, and the race has long been on to redefine zombies and find new ways to make them interesting, frightening, or even lovable. Dan Waters' *Generation Dead* is a great example of taking the idea of the living dead into fresh, uncharted territory, and Corpse Fauna is nothing like it.

I asked myself if Corpse Fauna was still relevant.

The answer came in how easily I slipped back into writing the characters that inhabit these stories, how quickly my concern for them sprang back to life, and also in the fact that while there are some classic genre conventions at play in these stories, no one yet has told a zombie story quite like this one or taken the living dead to the places Corpse Fauna goes. The point of any story isn't necessarily how new or innovative it gets with its genre elements, but what it uses those genre elements to say about the world, about humanity. It matters how much the author and reader care about its characters more than how far the rug can be pulled out from under people's expectations. Although the latter is a good thing to do, and I think Corpse Fauna does it well.

At least I hope so on all those counts.

Fair warning, for twists and surprises, here there be tigers. When I first started writing Corpse Fauna, I set some basic ground rules intended to push these stories in a new direction. For example, the walking dead in Corpse Fauna cannot be killed by a shot to the head, infection is not transferred by a bite, and, as is revealed in this volume, the Corpse Fauna walking dead possess a weird and inexplicable (for now) trait unique in zombie lore.

To me, Corpse Fauna feels as fresh now as it did when I first started it.

ANOTHER CHANCE FOR THE UNDEAD

Zombies truly are hard to kill.

Corpse Fauna returned in two volumes published by Dark Quest Books, *The Dead Bear Witness* and *Tears of Blood*, each with a striking cover by the supremely talented Glen Ostrander. They received a positive reception and shambled along through the genre world for a time. The third volume, *The Dead in Their Masses*, was written and planned for publication, and Glen painted yet another horrifying masterpiece for the cover.

Then the world turned yet again.

For reasons upon which I won't speculate, the publisher of those editions ceased almost all communication, stopped paying royalties, and went underground. I stopped publication of the third book (and remain unsure to this day if it would ever have seen print anyway) and reclaimed my rights to books one and two.

Corpse Fauna was once again consigned to the morgue of dead projects.

Afterward, I moved on to new stories.

With two failed attempts to bring Corpse Fauna to realization under my belt, I decided to let the dead lie. There were enough zombie books in the world for those readers hungering for more tales of the walking dead, and maybe Corpse Fauna's time had passed. I wanted to tell other stories, try my hand at new genres and characters, and so I did. I left a door open in the back of my mind for the possibility of completing the series one day in the future and publishing the whole thing, maybe through Amazon for the sake of finality, to get to the end of the story. But I didn't. For a variety of reasons, I probably never would have. Corpse Fauna for the most part looked really dead this time.

Until, that is, Greg Schauer and Danielle Ackley-McPhail approached me about bringing the books back into print with eSpec Books.

Before I answered, I experienced all the same questions and doubts yet again.

I've moved on in my writing in many ways. Zombies no longer hold the same appeal for me they once did. They no longer hold the same appeal for many readers. And with the world yet even more changed since the last revival, did Corpse Fauna still hold any relevance? Thankfully, once again, I realized the stories are as much fun as they once were, and that what I loved best about these stories are the characters. I spent a lot of time with Cornell, Della, Birch, and a bunch of others readers will meet in the forthcoming volumes—and I missed them to some extent. Even more I felt I owed it to *them* to finish their story. I had always had a grand plan for how the varied Corpse Fauna characters would come together and reach their fates, and I could almost feel them asking me to bring them all the rest of the way home.

Thus, grateful for the opportunity to do so, here I am bringing the dead back to life once again with the expert help of eSpec Books.

I believe these characters still speak to the contemporary world, and in some ways, more now than they did in the past. The world has changed much and not all for the better. The push and pull to preserve individual freedom in a world ruled by vicious mob mentalities in particular seems more poignant now than in the past and sharp parallel to hordes of invading corpses. And there's more to come in the other stories.

So my heartfelt thanks to you, readers, who have picked up this book.

I hope you'll stay with us for the rest of the story and help me see it through to the end this time.

As for zombie lore at large, it's up to you to decide where Corpse Fauna falls in the grand chronicle of the living dead, but regardless, I hope you enjoy the journey.

—James Chambers,
June, 2011
Risen from the Grave / February 2019

PREVIEW OF

Corpse Fauna
Volume Two

TEARS OF BLOOD

TEARS OF BLOOD

IN THE SHADOW OF THE STRANGER
ONE

Vale spotted the stranger cutting the blazing horizon like a black blade, a tall man striding unaccosted through an amber-tinted orchard of restless corpses. Sunset made a mad jumble of the shadows, but where the stranger walked there emerged a sort of order. The dead made way for him. They fell into ranks like rough soldiers at attention, framing serrations against the fiery sky before drifting back to a lethargic chaos after he passed. A hundred yards out from the barbed-wire perimeter, the stranger shifted toward the airport and crossed through the overgrown grass. Gazing down from the air traffic control tower, Vale watched him through binoculars.

The stranger looked like a weary traveler coming to the end of a long, grimy trail; a wanderer in black, mud-spattered slacks and a threadbare white shirt. His torn leather jacket flapped from his narrow shoulders like a battlefield standard. Vale thought he must be dead to walk through a field infested with wormfeeders without igniting a feeding frenzy, but he didn't look dead. He didn't move like the dead—stiff and aimless—nor did he resemble them—gray and blemished with rot. His bright eyes were focused on the path before him, and his cheeks burned red in the dry, gritty wind.

He stopped at the barbed-wire coils staked to the ground. The low sun cast his silhouette through the loops of razor-edged steel, through the chain-link fence behind them, and onto the high, dusty grass between the runways. When the stranger raised a hand to push the hair from his eyes, the shadow of his fingers reached for the terminal like a crow's beak. Then, with a shrug, he resumed walking along the perimeter toward the makeshift guardhouse, where Duncan and Tomaselli were on duty.

Vale snatched up her walkie-talkie to warn them but hesitated. She didn't know what to make of the stranger. Tourists simply didn't exist these days. The last had come more than nine weeks ago, driving a beat-up U.S. Postal Service delivery truck; sick, starved, and dehydrated, he'd died the same day, and they'd burned his corpse so he wouldn't become a wormfeeder. Since then, only the dead came. They looked through the fence with inexplicable eyes that stared from their arms and legs, from their torsos, necks, and hands. Their idiot moans chased the quiet from the night, and their stench poisoned the air. Most of the people sheltering in the airport believed they were the last of the living in the area, and Vale couldn't imagine where the stranger had hidden or how he'd survived on his own. *Maybe he really is dead,* she thought. Maybe her eyes were tricking her in the twilight. But, no, the way he'd stopped and pushed the hair from his face was a gesture only a living man would make.

She raised Tomaselli on the walkie-talkie. Standing orders required them to burn any of the dead who strayed too near the gate, and with the setting sun at his back, the stranger would be easily mistaken for a wormfeeder.

Tomaselli's voice came back: "We see him, Vale. We're not blind."

"Don't cook him," she said. "He's a tourist."

After a pause, Tomaselli said, "You positive?"

"I didn't take his pulse," Vale said, "but he sure as hell looks alive."

"Why aren't the dead tearing him to pieces?"

"I don't know."

"Doesn't matter," Tomsaelli said. "Alive or not, no one's coming through that gate except Campbell and his team. If they ever make it back."

"*When* they make it back," Vale said.

"They should've been here already. Dark soon." Tomaselli gave a humorless chuckle. "Only people outside after dark are fools and the dead, and all the fools died a long time ago."

"Anything on the radio?"

"Dead air and static."

Vale grimaced. The prospect of losing Campbell, of him becoming one of the walking dead, disgusted her. He had pulled the surviving airport people back together after Morgan almost destroyed them, and they were counting on him to lead them through the worst of what was to come. If Campbell didn't return, the little hope left among them would falter and die. Vale didn't want to even contemplate who would fill the vacuum Campbell's absence would leave. She whispered a wish for his safety, but the stranger's arrival was a bad omen.

"Vale? You got us covered?" Tomaselli said. "He's almost here."

"I'm on him," Vale said. "You'll get a closer look than me. Do what you have to do, but keep in mind if you torch him, you're probably burning him alive."

"Don't get your panties in a wad. We won't be inviting him in for dinner, but that doesn't mean we're going to roast his ass."

Vale signed off, set down her walkie-talkie, and then swapped her binoculars for the scope on the .50 caliber rifle mounted in the tower. Wind whistled across the open window in front of the gun. Vale placed the stranger in her crosshairs and rested her finger on the trigger. The rifle felt like an extension of her hands and eyes, like she could reach down through it across any distance and touch the stranger or anything else she saw. At her best, she could take the man out with a single shot to his spine, immobilizing him, her aim so accurate and sure she sometimes spooked the others, which was why no one minded how much time she spent in the tower. She settled into the shooting nest and tracked her target as he moved into the glare of the guardhouse floodlights.

The stranger cupped a hand over his eyes and stopped outside the gate. The chain-link barrier was mounted on wheels and reinforced with sheet metal and fuselage scraps torn from the dead, metal birds that littered the airport. The ground before it was a black wash of charred earth. The stranger stood at the center of the dead zone. Wind snapped the ragged hem of his coat. He glanced over his shoulder at the charnel mob then heeled around and peered through the chinks in the barrier. Nothing else stirred but the biting wind and the restless dead spread across the darkening meadow.

When Duncan emerged from the guard shack with a shotgun braced against his hip, Vale exhaled and caressed the trigger, ready to fire. His cap pulled low over mirrored sunglasses, Duncan approached the gate. Vale knew he would turn the man away. Everyone at the airport had agreed they would take in no more tourists, not after what had happened back before the perimeter was erected—back when there were more than a hundred of them instead of only eighteen. That was Morgan's fault, and now Morgan and so many of the others walked with the dead. Some days, Vale saw Morgan in her sights and thought about putting him down, but she preferred not to waste the ammunition. She wouldn't hesitate, though, to spend a round on the stranger if he became a threat.

Vale read Duncan's body language: *Go away. You're not welcome here.*

The stranger stayed.

He looked at the fading sky then turned back to the gate, waiting. A ghost noise hummed in Vale's ears, a phantom vibration that ran through the tower and into her body. She risked a glance east toward Actsburg.

Beyond the runways and the meadow, on the far side of the concrete loops of the highway, lay the dim and lifeless city, sprawling like a spent lover between the airport and the wild, gray ocean. Vale saw nothing there. The hum became a buzz, then a faint rumble. Vale snatched up her walkie-talkie to check in with Tomaselli, but the crack of gunshots snapped her attention back to the meadow. The rumble became the growl of a motor, and Vale sighted on the airport access road. Cresting a hill, an armored pick-up truck sped into view, jolting over cracked pavement as it slalomed through rows of shambling corpses.

Campbell was back.

Vale watched him through her scope. Hunched in the truck bed amidst crammed-in boxes and packages, he clutched a rifle and fired at the dead swarming toward him.

TWO

Putrefying wormfeeders ruptured when the truck smashed into them with the metal T-bar affixed to its front bumper. The ram bristled with jagged bits of scrap metal welded onto it. Blood and entrails painted it black and purple. Torn-flesh streamers flapped from the fenders and a scalp, dangling by a thread of knotted hair and leathery skin, bobbed in front of the license plate. The body of the truck, armored with pieces from a 747's skin, was mottled with smears of blood and clumps of gore. *Dawson's going to be pissed when Campbell returns it to the garage,* Vale thought. It would take days to clean. But that didn't matter. *Campbell was back.*

His rifle popped with a sound like hail pattering on a car roof. Vale felt the urge to open fire on the dead in the truck's path, but her duty was to cover the gate. She couldn't risk taking her eyes off the stranger for more than a few seconds. He was inching closer to the entrance despite Duncan poking his shotgun through a slit in the armor and yelling at him to go away. Tomaselli came from the guardhouse with a flamethrower strapped on his back and climbed to the top of the ten-foot-high scaffolding that served as the fire post. He crouched there, behind a sheet metal barrier topped with barbed wire and lit the flamethrower's nozzle. Its fiery tongue lashed the dusk.

The truck jounced off the road into the well-worn ruts of a shortcut across the meadow. Excited by the activity, the wormfeeders were converging fast on the pick-up. It wouldn't be long before enough of them gathered to stop it. The truck surged past them, ran over them, and Campbell shot. Here and there, the dead fell. A single bullet couldn't destroy them, but Campbell tried to hobble their feet and legs. "Kneecapping the dead," they called it. Firing from a moving vehicle, he was lucky to hit the very few he did, but how the dead mobbed together made it hard to miss completely as long as he aimed low and fired often. Vale wondered why only Campbell was shooting. Burnett was probably driving, so Reading should've been riding shotgun.

The dusk flared as Tomaselli triggered the flamethrower and burned the first of the wormfeeders to approach the gate. They always came in close when they sensed it was about to be opened. The flame ignited them and drove them back. Vale thought, if it came to it she might shoot the stranger to spare him being eaten alive, but the dead passed him by as if he wasn't there. Even as smoke spiraled around him, rising from the dead zone, where the cinders wouldn't ignite, the stranger stood his ground, serene, unshaken. As if he were somehow immune to the chaos all around him. A chill ran through Vale, and she wondered if this was how she looked to the others when they saw her shooting the dead with cold, mechanical accuracy.

The truck zigzagged around the thickest groups of wormfeeders, bounced hard over a low hill, and Campbell tumbled out of sight in the cargo bed. Moments later, he was up again, hanging onto the side, struggling to get back into shooting position. The truck swerved toward the gate, sending him off balance again. Smoke from the burning wormfeeders corkscrewed in its wind as it crashed through the last line of the dead and broke clear for the entrance.

Vale refreshed her aim on the stranger.

In a flurry of motion, Duncan raised the bracing bar, withdrew his gun, and rolled the creaking gate wide. The truck sped through. Rubber bit pavement. Brakes screeched as the vehicle skidded to a stop. Duncan slammed the gate shut behind it and clasped the lock. The routine was well-practiced and there hadn't been any wasted motion—but still Duncan had proven too slow.

The stranger stood inside the barrier.

Vale blinked.

She had seen the man in her scope one moment, gone the next, but she hadn't seen him move. She put him back in her sight, and she ought to have fired then, but an overwhelming feeling that it would be a mistake stayed her trigger finger. The stranger didn't present an immediate threat. He only stood still and watched the other men with calm, fearless eyes until Tomaselli aimed the torch at him, and then he simply sat cross-legged on the concrete, placed his hands palms-up on his knees, and bowed his head. Vale thought she understood, given his options of crossing back through the crowds of the dead or taking his chances with living people. Yet, as unthreatening as he seemed, there was something to his posture, to how he moved that set Vale's hairs on end.

Without noticing the stranger, Campbell clambered down from the pick-up bed then reached back and dragged a bundle onto the tailgate, knocking a box to the road, where it broke and spilled out cans of food. The cans rolled and scattered, forcing Burnett to step around them as he rushed from the driver's seat to help Campbell ease Reading to the ground. His clothes were soaked with blood. Campbell began CPR, while Burnett tried to use Reading's blood-sopped shirt to pack a wet gash in his midriff where loops of pale, gray intestine peeked out. Putting the stranger back in her sight, Vale radioed the terminal to send Farley, the paramedic who'd become their doctor. It would take him minutes to reach the gate. Vale didn't think that would be soon enough. Campbell's upper body fell and rose with each compression, but Reading looked so pale, Vale couldn't imagine there was barely more than a drop of blood left in him.

A distant car motor coughed to life then rumbled as Farley's compact started on the far side of the terminal.

He was already too late.

Burnett dropped the bloodstained shirt and gripped Campbell's arm. Campbell stopped the chest compressions. Reading's blood pooled around him in a growing sheet as it hemorrhaged from a wound that had been much too big, much too deep. Burnett checked his watch then signaled the start of the countdown. Campbell unholstered his pistol, and Tomaselli stood ready with the torch. Duncan and Burnett drew their guns. And while they were distracted by the shock of Reading's death, the stranger leapt up and rushed past them to the body.

He knelt by Reading's shoulders. Campbell, Tomaselli, Vale— any one of them should've blown him away then and there, but they were too stunned to react and the stranger moved so fast it was hard to follow him. The gaunt man set one hand on Reading's forehead and caressed his empty eyes shut. He lowered his head, shoulders swaying while he blessed Reading with the sign of the cross. After that, he stepped away and raised his hands in surrender.

Duncan dragged him off the tarmac and shoved him to the dirt. The stranger tried to get up, but Duncan prodded the back of his neck with his shotgun to keep him down. Unsure of what she'd witnessed, Vale kept the stranger in her scope, telling herself he was trouble, that she should take the shot, take him out—and yet she couldn't make herself fire. From the back of her mind, the voice that had helped her stay alive since the day she left her apartment told her the stranger was somehow important, that he was necessary, although for what, she had no idea. Burnett waved for Tomaselli to torch Reading's body. The stranger pleaded with them to wait. He tried to shove himself in front of the flamethrower, but Duncan kicked him back. From the tower, it was like watching a silent movie with everyone waving their hands, and their faces drawn in exaggerated expressions, their shouts silent across the distance. Tomaselli pointed the barrel of the torch at Reading, but then, like Vale, he faltered. Vale wondered if he sensed, as she did, that there was something extraordinary about the stranger.

Two minutes passed.

Seconds ticked by.

Another minute, then two. Reading should have risen.

The threshold for reanimation passed, and the world seemed to sputter except for the keening winds and the drone of Farley's approaching car.

Reading didn't rise.

His eyes didn't flutter open, nor did his body spasm and snap upright; his black, blood-caked mouth didn't grind to life with a hunger for hot blood and human flesh. His lips stayed shut tight. All the men at the checkpoint—except Duncan—lowered their weapons and stared at Reading's corpse.

Campbell's voice crackled over Vale's walkie-talkie. "Vale, you got this tourist in your sights?"

"Tight on him," she said.

"Figured you would've capped him by now."

"So did I," she said. "But it didn't seem like the right move. There's something about this guy, Campbell."

"What is it?"

"I don't know. A feeling."

"Good or bad, darling?"

Vale considered the question then said, "Neither. Only that...he matters. You should've seen him cross the meadow. He was like a ghost. The wormfeeders cleared a path for him. And what he did to Reading... If he can stop the dead from rising then I'm not sure we should hurt him or turn him away until we understand how he's doing these things."

Vale watched Campbell, his long shadow stretching into the gloom while he thought. She admired how he weighed what he knew, considered all the angles, and yet could still make snap decisions when needed. It was a quality that had saved lives and earned him Vale's trust.

"Goddamn funny thing is," he came back, "I got the same feeling. Except maybe for Duncan, so do the others. Everyone's hair's on end."

"Where's this guy from?" Vale asked. "Has he said anything?"

"Only that he's here to help us, that all he wants is shelter. Says we're in danger."

"I could've told you that," Vale said.

"Listen, I want to take this guy in and talk to him but on my terms. We don't need another riot and public display of stupidity. He goes to the pen in Hangar Four, not to the terminal. We'll hear what he has to say then decide what to do with him."

"The others won't like it," Vale said.

"Let them bitch," Campbell said. "Turns out this guy has nothing to offer, I'll cast him out myself, and they'll never even meet him. But I need your help. Anything goes the slightest bit wonky, if he lays a hand on any one of us down here, tries to make a signal, or moves for a weapon, for anything, you shoot this bastard to pieces. I'm not fucking kidding. Got it?"

"Not a problem," Vale said. "Be careful."

Campbell approached the stranger, who stood under guard between Duncan and Tomaselli, and then without warning punched him square in the face. The stranger's head snapped back, and he crumpled to the ground. Campbell struck him twice more on the back of the head and then kicked the man until he lay face down on the concrete and stopped trying to get up. Campbell jabbed a knee against the stranger's back, pinning him while he went through his pockets and clothing. He found nothing. Burnett and Duncan tied the stranger's hands, and then they loaded him into the truck and climbed on after him, squeezing in with the goods packed there. The stranger sat in the truck bed, head tilted upward as if he was admiring the beauty of the blazing sunset, and Vale wondered how he could be so peaceful and brave after being beaten and bound. Campbell slid into the driver's seat, and then the vehicle rolled away. Vale watched it pass Farley's car as the medic parked along the edge of the road. Then she relaxed and lifted her eye from her gun's scope.

Farley got out of the battered compact. He nudged Reading's body with his foot then gave it a cursory check. Afterward, he collected the fallen cans and wiped them off on the grass before he stacked them back into their broken box. He carried the box to his car and, once he was clear, Tomaselli showered Reading with flame. The corpse ignited in a shimmering wave of heat and a cloud of smoke that added to the haze from the burning wormfeeders. The tower stood downwind. Vale tugged the bandanna around her neck up over her mouth and nose and looked away. The flesh of someone really dead, someone who hadn't been resurrected, smelled very different when it burned. It was an odor she'd never get used to. She watched the pick-up truck cut left across a runway toward Hangar Four then checked the clock she kept propped up on the blank radar display.

One hour left in her shift.

One hour left to watch the dead.

THREE

In darkness, Vale crossed the derelict tarmac riddled with weeds; the chill wind ferreted out the gaps and bare spots in her clothing, but the cold and solitude suited her. She felt weary enough to go crash at her sleeping place in the international departures lounge, but at the same time, she was too curious and wired to sleep. She hiked toward Hangar Four with her Ruger Mini-14 in her hands. At least there she could avoid another night of sitting around the terminal, listening to everyone pining for the world to go back to how it had been before the dead walked.

Vale's fingers and toes were numb when she reached the hangar. She slung her Ruger across her back and pushed through the door. The pen stood under rows of lights at the opposite end of the otherwise empty space. A breeze whistled across the building's upper reaches. Armed with shotguns, Burnett and Duncan lingered on the fringes of the lighted circle around the pen. They nodded as Vale passed them. A generator hummed outside, and when the wind slacked, the moans of the dead reached even here.

The pen was an ugly but sturdy cage cobbled together from fence scraps, reinforced with strips of metal from the scavenged jets and laced with lengths of razor wire dangerous to anyone inside it that didn't keep toward its center. The stranger sat there on a desk chair with one broken arm. On the other side of the wall, Campbell sat across from him, looking worn out yet unflinching as he returned the prisoner's stare. Vale guessed the interrogation had gone sour.

Bad shit to deal with after losing Reading.

"So?" Vale said. "What's his story?"

"Not much of a conversationalist, this one," Campbell said. "Tells me we've lost our way, and he wants to set us back upon a righteous path. Apparently our souls are in as much danger as our bodies. Fucking head case."

"He have a name?"

"Everyone has a name," Campbell said. "He's keeping his to himself."

Something about the stranger nagged at Vale. His eyes were deep and tranquil, and when she looked into his face, a warm, friendly feeling came over her. It made her uncomfortable. The stranger smiled. She turned away.

She said, "What happened to Reading?"

Campbell sighed. "We were overrun. The dead were in the storeroom at Food Wizard. We tried to go out the back, but they were in the alley, too, so we cut through the pharmacy next door. We stood in the front window and let them see us, trying to draw them to that spot so we could make a run for it out the side door.

One of the plate glass windows gave out under about fifty or so wormfeeders. A big shard of it tore through Reading. He was standing between it and me. Probably saved my life. I got him to the truck while the dead were still picking themselves up, but we barely made it out of town. They were everywhere, more than I've ever seen at one time before."

"Reading was a good man."

"Yes, he was."

"How'd this guy stop him from rising?" Vale asked.

Campbell shrugged. "He won't say."

He stood up, gestured for Vale to follow him, and then they left Burnett and Duncan to watch the prisoner. Vale trailed Campbell through the dark expanse to an office used as guards' quarters when the pen was occupied. Campbell lit an electric lantern and hung it from a coat rack. In the shaky light he took Vale in his arms and kissed her. He smelled of sweat and dust and blood. Driven by relief that he was still alive, Vale responded, her fingertips dallying at the back of his skull. Then she broke away. She knew where this would lead, and she didn't want to go there. Not again. Not now, anyway, and certainly not in this place.

Vale glimpsed the hurt in Campbell's eyes as he turned away and flopped onto a chair behind the desk, but when he spun around to face her, his expression was as strong and focused as she'd ever seen it. She had told him she wanted time, but she hadn't told him that she regretted what they'd done, that she saw no point in relationships. They'd only ever held her back in the past, and she didn't see how they could last in the present or the future. Her perspective set her apart from the other airport people, who believed that all they really had left was each other. She wondered if Campbell understood. She wondered how long he might wait for her to come around or if she ever would.

"Food Wizard is pretty much picked clean," Campbell said. "We got the last of the canned stuff out of the warehouse today. We'll get the rest of the bottled water next time. Then Corrigan's going to hit the medical supply store across town. After that all we need is more camping equipment, batteries, clothing, and we're ready to move."

"Another week or two, then," Vale said.

"Give or take," Campbell said. "I miss Marcus. We'd be done by now if we still had a pilot."

Marcus had taken people on forays into town in the helicopter parked on the other side of the airport, but he'd died in Morgan's disaster and left them earthbound. Later they found him wandering along the fence and because everyone had liked Marcus, they burned his corpse to bone and ash.

"You still sure this is the right time to go?" Vale asked.

"What do you mean?"

"We've got a good thing here at least as far as shelter and security. It isn't perfect, but we can sleep safe and sound most nights. Why not ride out the cold weather here and head out come spring?"

"We won't last the winter here," Campbell said. "Food will be scarce by New Year's. Making it into Actsburg and back won't be possible on icy, snow-packed roads that no one will ever plow. The generators will die before February unless we turn up another tanker of gas, and good luck with that. You've seen how everyone is. They're past being on their last nerve. And, damn me for admitting it, but so am I. If you're sleeping soundly at night, you're the only one. You think being cooped up here three, four more months, while we run out of everything, and the days get short and dark that one or more of us isn't going to snap? Then what? We start attacking each other? Or someone opens a gate in the middle of the night and lets the wormfeeders in?"

Vale flopped onto a creaky office chair and checked the clip in her Ruger. Campbell was right. Waiting would gain them nothing but misery. It didn't matter where they went; they couldn't stay here.

"Last I knew you were itching to be out of here more than any of us. Onward, upward, and don't look back. That's your philosophy, right? Now you're sounding like Morgan's right-hand asshole," Campbell said.

"Don't even mention that moron in the same breath as me," Vale said. "I'm nothing like him."

"No. You're not. He was in a category of one. I'm sorry," Campbell said. "But that doesn't change anything. We won't last the winter here."

"It was a passing thought, is all," Vale said. "I'm not thinking straight. That tourist out there screws with my head."

"I know. It's how he stares you down," Campbell said. "Makes you want to trust him. Makes you doubt yourself. You're right, there's something to him. He matters in a weird way. But I can't figure out how, and he's not offering much insight."

"Maybe he's mad you punched him the face," Vale said.

"And also the back of the head before I kicked him. Yeah, guess I'd be pissed off too if I were him." Campbell rubbed his eyes then slouched in his chair. "I don't like it. You know that, right? I don't like being hard like this, using violence as my default position. It's not who I am or who I want to be. I wish things could be different. All the bad things I do are only because I don't see that I have a choice."

"I know that," Vale said. "It's us or them, life or death, and we do what we have to do. We all wish things could be different. But you know what? I bet we all wished that even before the dead started walking."

"True," Campbell said. "But as much as I complained about how shitty I had it back then, I'd trade the dead plague for my bitchy ex-wife and too much overtime in a heartbeat. I guess we all would."

"Maybe." Vale shrugged. "Sometimes people get what they wish for."

Campbell pushed his hair back and yawned. "I should let this guy rest tonight," Campbell said. "Try him again tomorrow with a clearer head."

"Get some sleep," Vale said. "You need it."

"Vale, listen, don't lose hope. Even with the roads as bad as they are, we can make it down the coast in two or three weeks once we leave here. Another few days to make our way inland and we're home and warm. My uncle's farm was still running when I was there last year. Even if he and his family are all gone, there'll be food from last season's harvest, maybe livestock and supplies. All we have to do is raise some barriers, ride out a soft winter, and then come spring we'll make ourselves self-sustaining. It'll be better there. Everyone will be so busy working to survive they won't have time to crack up. As long as we start out in another month, we'll beat the really cold weather. So hang in there."

Before Vale could respond, a hollow, rasping voice interjected from the darkness outside the office: "Anyone who's still here tomorrow night will die and become one of the walking dead."

Campbell and Vale erupted from their seats, grabbing their guns as they rose, and faced the stranger standing framed in the black rectangle of the doorway. His cracked lips curled in a ghost grin; his hands hung at his sides, palms out, facing Vale and Campbell. A deep, black spot, like an ancient scab, marred the center of each one. With the shadows falling across his face, the stranger's eyes looked like steel pellets. Vale lowered her weapon. She couldn't help it. She already knew she wasn't going to shoot him.

"How the fuck did you get loose?" Campbell rushed across the office, waving his gun in the stranger's face. "On your knees! Now!"

The stranger complied. Campbell slipped behind him and pushed the mouth of his gun against the back of the man's skull. Then he leaned out into the void of the hangar and called for Burnett and Duncan. When the echo of his voice died, the darkness returned only whispers—and the faint sound of... crying?

"Hold him here," Campbell said. Vale hesitated, and Campbell's face reddened. "Vale, put your fucking gun against his head and make sure he goes nowhere."

Campbell's tone jarred Vale. She took up her position. The stranger seemed unconcerned by the touch of her gun at his back. Campbell walked into gloom of the hangar. His voice reverberated as he called to the others. Vale watched his shadow cut the glow from the lights around the pen, and then he fell out of sight when he rounded the cage. Faint voices came through the darkness: Campbell, Burnett, Duncan. More whispers, too soft to reach Vale.

A shotgun blast rocked the hangar.

Vale jolted and squeezed her gun.

"No! What the hell?" Campbell shouted. "Duncan! Drop it!"

"Campbell!" Vale called.

No answer.

A lamp clanked, flashed as it teetered, then fell and cast a whirl of shadows before it smashed on the ground. Duncan howled. Campbell shouted something raw. Vale heard a scuffle. She seized the stranger by his jacket and tugged him onto his feet. With her gun jabbed against the base of his neck, she marched him toward the pen.

"Campbell?" she called. "You all right?"

The sound of flesh smacking flesh came in three short bursts. Duncan cried out. Vale's pulse raced. She stroked the trigger of her Ruger as she steered the stranger into the illuminated zone. Duncan was on his knees, clutching his head, tears streaming down his cheeks. Blood ran from a gash beneath his right eye. Burnett lay behind him, most of his skull and brain splattered across the floor. His shotgun lay next to him. The door to the pen hung open. Campbell stood over Duncan, holding the sobbing man's shotgun in one hand, his other bloodied from punching Duncan's face. Duncan's sunglasses lay in pieces on the ground.

"Oh, god," Vale said. "What happened?"

"They were standing here, crying, and then...he shot him! Duncan shot Burnett," Campbell told her. "Then... he tried to kill himself."

The stranger rushed away from Vale and crouched next to Burnett's body, where he said a prayer and made the same gestures that had spared Reading existence as a wormfeeder. Campbell proved less forgiving this time. He stormed forward and raked the stranger's head with the butt of Duncan's shotgun, knocking him down.

"What did you say to them?" Campbell kicked the stranger in the stomach, and then furious, he turned to Vale, and said, "They released him. They opened the fucking lock and let him go. He talked them into it, convinced them there was no point in holding him, no point in going on living, or some kind of bullshit. Burnett said he wanted to die, and then Duncan just turned and...he just...fired. There was nothing I could do.

Burnett didn't even try to move. He let it happen, like he really did want it."

Campbell whirled and dragged Duncan to his feet.

"Why'd you do it?" he said. "What's wrong with you?"

Duncan trembled. His breaths came fast and shallow, and when he tried to speak his lips quivered, and he said only, "I...I...I...I...." Vale thought he might be going into shock. Campbell repeated his question, shouting, but Duncan couldn't answer. Campbell shoved him into the pen and then locked the door. He stepped back to the stranger and kicked him in the ribs. The stranger jerked sideways, tumbled away from Campbell, and then pushed himself off the floor and sat up, indifferent to the beating.

"What did you say to them?" Campbell shouted.

"I told them what I was about to tell you." The stranger's voice resonated, like a cello string holding a long, deep note. It penetrated Vale, impossible to deny; its power made her shiver. "I didn't mean for this man to kill his friend, but death comes to us all, and there's no predicting when or where, even as there's no predicting how anyone will react to the truth. Sometimes the truth has unintended consequences. Both hope and despair can rob a man of his soul. We make our choices alone. These two men were not prepared to hear the truth. Maybe you aren't either."

"What the hell does that mean?" Campbell said. He grabbed the stranger by the shoulders and thrashed him. "Who are you? Why'd you come here? Tell me!"

Campbell shoved the stranger across the floor. The man rolled into a bank of lights that clattered to the ground and shattered. A narrow arc of illumination came from the one remaining lamp. Campbell raised the shotgun over his head like a club and surged after the stranger. Vale bolted between them and forced Campbell back. He tried to yank free of her, but she refused to let him go. Knowing he'd never hit her, she coaxed him away from the stranger, step by step, and then she slid her arm around his back and held him, stroking his head, until the razor edge of his anger dulled.

She understood his rage. Burnett and Campbell were friends from the old world, and losing him and Reading in a matter of hours had dropped their number to sixteen—thirteen men, three women. And the stranger—but Vale didn't see much chance of him filling anyone's spot. They needed three trucks to carry all the food and supplies bound for the farm, twelve people to man the trucks and guns in shifts, and then there would be casualties after they left the airport perimeter. The fewer people there were, the less their chances of survival. The cold calculus of the situation flashed through Vale's mind, even as she saw Campbell reaching the same conclusion. The plan he believed in, the plan he wanted Vale and everyone else to believe in, was in danger of falling victim to a crazy man spreading madness among Campbell's people. He couldn't allow it. He pumped the gun to clear the shell Duncan had fired and reload the chamber. Then he circled around the stranger and prepared to execute him.

ABOUT THE AUTHOR

James Chambers is an award-winning author of horror, crime, fantasy, and science fiction. He wrote the Bram Stoker Award®-winning graphic novel, *Kolchak the Night Stalker: The Forgotten Lore of Edgar Allan Poe* and was nominated for a Bram Stoker Award for his story, "A Song Left Behind in the Aztakea Hills." *Publisher's Weekly* gave his collection of four Lovecraftian-inspired novellas, *The Engines of Sacrifice*, a starred review and described it as "...chillingly evocative."

He is the author of the short story collections *On the Night Border* and *Resurrection House* and several novellas, including *The Dead Bear Witness*, *Tears of Blood*, and *The Dead in Their Masses*, in the Corpse Fauna novella series, and the dark urban fantasy, *Three Chords of Chaos*.

His short stories have been published in numerous anthologies, including *After Punk: Steampowered Tales of the Afterlife*, *The Best of Bad-Ass Faeries*, *The Best of Defending the Future*, *Chiral Mad 2*, *Chiral Mad 4*, *Deep Cuts*, *Dragon's Lure*, *Fantastic Futures 13*, *Footprints in the Stars*, *Gaslight and Grimm*, *The Green Hornet Chronicles*, *Hardboiled Cthulhu*, *Heroes of the Realm*, *In An Iron Cage*, *In Harm's Way*, *Kolchak the Night Stalker: Passages of the Macabre*, *The Pulp Horror Book of Phobias*, *Qualia Nous*, *Shadows Over Main Street* (1 and 2), *The Spider: Extreme Prejudice*, *To Hell in a Fast Car*, *Truth or Dare*, *TV Gods*, *Walrus*

Tales, Weird Trails; the chapbook *Mooncat Jack*; and the magazines *Bare Bone, Cthulhu Sex,* and *Allen K's Inhuman.*

He co-edited the anthology, *A New York State of Fright: Horror Stories from the Empire State*, which received a Bram Stoker Award nomination.

He has also written and edited numerous comic books including *Leonard Nimoy's Primortals*, the critically acclaimed "The Revenant" in *Shadow House*, and *The Midnight Hour* with Jason Whitley.

He is a member of the Horror Writers Association and recipient of the 2012 Richard Laymon Award and the 2016 Silver Hammer Award.

He lives in New York.

Visit his website: www.jameschambersonline.com.

ABOUT THE ARTIST

Glen Ostrander (cover) is a Freelance Artist and Illustrator who has created artwork in the fantasy/horror genre for a wide variety of commercial clients. He is known for his evocative work and continues to bring his creations to life by finding daily inspiration near his home, in the wild mountains of New Hampshire, where he lives with his wonderful wife Anna, his devilish dog Jojo, and his fiendish feline Floyd.

Jason Whitley (interior) is the illustrator and co-creator of *The Midnight Hour*. Jason's work as a newspaper illustrator has appeared across the country and won many awards. His portrait of civil rights leader Charlotte Hawkins Brown is in the Charlotte Hawkins Brown Museum. With writer Scott Eckelaert, he co-created and illustrated the classic comic-strip, *Sea Urchins. Sea Urchins* has been collected into four volumes. The fourth volume, So Long, Frozen Ocean will be released in 2020. Jason leads a Hermes and Telly Award-winning multimedia team of five in North Carolina. He's working on a crime-noir graphic novel with no set release date and looking forward to the complete *The Midnight Hour* collection from eSpec Books in 2020.